HER BOSS'S
ONE-NIGHT BABY

HER BOSS'S ONE-NIGHT BABY

JENNIE LUCAS

MILLS & BOON

First published in Great Britain 2020
by Mills & Boon, an imprint of HarperCollins*Publishers*
1 London Bridge Street, London, SE1 9GF

Large Print edition 2020

© 2020 Jennie Lucas

ISBN: 978-0-263-08471-9

This book is produced from independently certified
FSC™ paper to ensure responsible forest management. For
more information visit www.harpercollins.co.uk/green.

Printed and bound in Great Britain
by CPI Group (UK) Ltd, Croydon, CR0 4YY

CHAPTER ONE

SOFT PINK CLOUDS glowed between modern sky-scrapers as the sun rose over Tokyo. It was early April, and white-and-pink cherry blossoms covered the trees like wedding confetti, as joyful and sweet as a first kiss.

But Hana Everly barely noticed. She stared out the window of the Rolls-Royce, her heart pounding, her skin in a cold sweat.

"And find a new housekeeper for my penthouse in New York, to replace Mrs. Stone..."

Her boss's low growl came beside her in the back seat as he tersely listed other tasks he needed her to handle immediately—if not sooner. Hana's pen moved listlessly, but his words barely registered. She took a shuddering breath.

She couldn't be pregnant.

Couldn't be.

They'd been careful. And her boss had been clear about the rules. Even as his hot, sensual lips had kissed her, his voice had murmured against her skin, "One night, nothing more. There will be no romance, no marriage. No consequences. Tomorrow you will be my assistant again, I your employer. Do you agree?"

Such a deal with the devil, and yet she'd whispered, "Yes."

Hana would have agreed to anything then, when he'd had her spread across his bed, experiencing such intoxicating sensuality for the first time. But even that hadn't been enough. He'd pulled back to look at her, his black eyes cold, even cruel.

"You will leave my bed before dawn, Hana, and neither of us will ever speak of this again. Even to each other."

Lost in a haze of pleasure, she'd nodded, and with a heavy-lidded smile, Antonio had lowered his head to plunder her lips with a sizzling kiss.

She'd thought she knew what she was doing. At the age of twenty-six, she'd told herself she could handle sex without commitment. Because Antonio Delacruz could never be her boyfriend. He was her boss, the ruthless billionaire CEO and largest shareholder of the world's fastest-growing airline. There was a reason that Cross-World Airways was crushing its competitors.

Antonio stopped at nothing to get what he wanted.

But he hadn't been the one to cross this line.

She'd been the one who'd kissed him first. She still couldn't believe she'd done it. But when he'd found her crying, late one night in his *palacio* in Madrid, he'd taken her into his arms to comfort her.

And at that, two years of repressed, pent-up desire had exploded inside Hana. Shocking even herself, she'd lifted on her tiptoes and kissed him through her tears. It had been the barest whisper of a kiss. Terrified at her own boldness, she'd started to pull away.

Then he'd stopped her, pulling her back swiftly into his arms…

For the last two months, Hana had tried not to remember that night in Madrid. She'd tried to be modern about it. She'd tried to forget, as Antonio obviously had.

But now it seemed her body would not let her. The single night of hot, raw, shocking pleasure between Hana and her handsome, arrogant, rich-beyond-imagination boss would be one she'd live with forever. Because she was going to have his baby.

As the sedan drove north through Tokyo in

the cool morning, Hana put her clammy hand to her cheek, feeling dizzy with morning sickness and fear. Her baby would grow up with no father or worse—a bad father. Because Antonio Delacruz hadn't become rich by caring about other people. He'd won by being ruthless. He had no family and, in the two years she'd worked for him, his longest love affair had lasted six weeks. Not that she'd been paying attention.

A lump rose in her throat. This wasn't how she'd imagined having a baby. Her plan had been to get married, settle down and *then* get pregnant.

This was wrong, all wrong. She didn't even have a home. She couldn't raise a child like her parents had raised her, always on the move, never staying long enough to build roots, yanking Hana out of each place the moment she started to make real friends.

The lump in her throat turned to a razor blade. She never should have slept with Antonio, no matter how incredible it had felt in the moment. She should have waited for a real relationship, a committed one. She should never, ever have sought comfort in Antonio's arms, placing her whole future, and her unborn baby's future, in his careless hands—

"Hana?" her boss demanded acidly beside her in the back seat of the Rolls-Royce. "Hello?"

"Yes," she said. Numbly, she looked down at her notes. "You want the SWOT analysis for the expansion into Australia, the numbers from the Berlin office, hire a new housekeeper for New York and arrange the after-party in London."

He stared at her for a long moment with his deep black eyes, and she felt a shiver of fear. But not even Antonio Delacruz, the fearsome billionaire with the mysterious past who'd built a worldwide empire from nothing, had the ability to read minds.

At least she prayed he didn't. Otherwise, she was in big trouble.

"Good," he said grudgingly. He looked back at his laptop screen. "And contact the lead architect on the new first-class lounge design for Heathrow…"

As the chauffeur drove them north toward the Marunouchi district, she fought her despair as she looked out at the glittering skyscrapers. She had visited Tokyo many times since she was a child. She loved this city, the place where her grandmother had been born before she'd emigrated to America. Her best friend Ren lived here, and the *sakura* season, or cherry-blooming season, was the most beautiful of the year.

But for once, the sight of Tokyo Tower, which looked like a bright red Eiffel Tower overlooking the city, did not make her heart rise. Even the lushly blooming trees did not cheer her. She was lost in her own panic.

There will be no romance, no marriage. No consequences. Neither of us will ever speak of this again. Even to each other. Do you agree?

Yes.

She'd never imagined their one night together could lead to a child. What should she do? Should she tell him? Could she?

Hana had only found out about the pregnancy a few hours ago, when she'd taken the test on their private jet from Madrid. But already, this child felt real. She placed her hand wondrously over the curve of her belly. *A baby.*

"What's wrong, Hana?" Antonio demanded beside her. "Why are you so distracted?"

Looking up with an intake of breath at the handsome Spaniard sitting beside her, she choked out, "Antonio, there's something I need to tell you."

The local driver and Ramon Garcia, the bodyguard who usually traveled with him, glanced at each other in the front seat. None of Mr. Delacruz's employees would dream of calling him by his first name. Aside from their night in bed, Hana had never taken such a liberty before. At least not out loud.

He looked at her coldly. "Yes, Miss Everly?"

His husky, slightly accented voice put her firmly in her place, reminding her—if she needed reminding—that she was his employee, nothing more.

Hana's soul quailed. They were nearly to the Marunouchi district, where a critical business negotiation waited. She and Antonio, along with the rest of the Tokyo-based team, had been prepping for this for months. Antonio was obsessed with negotiating a codeshare with Iyokan Airways, an important regional airline that would gain them routes to Tokyo, Osaka and beyond.

Maybe she should put off telling him about the baby for now.

Maybe she should put it off forever.

She pushed the traitorous thought aside. Even if Antonio rejected her and the baby outright, didn't he have the right to know? Didn't her baby at least deserve the chance to have a father?

"I need to tell you something," she whispered. She glanced uneasily toward the two men sitting in the front seat, who were pretending not to listen. "About…that night."

Antonio looked at her, his dark eyes like ice. "Which night is that?"

Did he truly not remember? His handsome face was so arrogant and cold, she almost wondered if the night he'd taken her virginity had been a dream. But the pregnancy test had left no doubt.

Hana lifted her chin and said clearly, "Our night together in Madrid. Two months ago."

The eyes of the men in the front seat went wide. Antonio calmly pressed the button to close the privacy screen between the front and back of the luxury sedan. Once it was closed, he turned on her fiercely.

"You promised never to talk about it."

"I know, but—"

"There's no *but*. You gave me your word."

"I have good reason—"

"I can imagine." His jaw clenched as he turned away. "You will put that night from your mind, Miss Everly. It never happened."

As the Rolls-Royce Phantom turned up the sweeping curve in front of a gleaming skyscraper overlooking the wide green-and-pink vistas of the East Gardens of the Imperial Palace, her voice was a squeak. "But—"

The car stopped, and a waiting doorman reached to open his door.

"It never happened," Antonio repeated, and without bothering to look at her, he swept out, all masculine power and hard muscular angles in his dark suit and sharply tailored black cashmere coat.

Pulling her handbag over her shoulder, Hana climbed out behind him numbly. Her heart was pounding. She held her notebook and briefcase tightly against her chest, as if they could protect her.

"Welcome, Mr. Delacruz," Emika Ito, the Tokyo team lead, greeted them in English with a respectful bow of her head. She was pretty, black-haired and chic. She smiled at Hana, who tried to smile back. "All is ready, sir."

Standing on the sidewalk, Hana glanced at the building. Inside the glass and steel lobby, she saw the rest of the lead team already assembled, waiting for their arrival so they could go to their new office on the top three floors.

"Yes, of course," Antonio said. "Thank you, Miss Ito. Give me a moment." With a nod, the girl returned to the lobby, leaving Hana and Antonio alone, with his bodyguard at a discreet distance. He looked down at her.

"So you agree?" he said tersely. It was intimate, having them so close together on the sidewalk in the cool spring morning. "It's forgotten?"

Hana felt a breeze against her hot cheek, saw a single cherry blossom floating and twisting in a tumult on the wind, before disappearing into the traffic of Hibiya Dori.

She couldn't tell him. She just couldn't. She'd nod and quietly go into the building, and be the assistant he needed during this important meeting. Afterward, she would quit. She would disappear. She bowed her head.

"Good," he said. She saw the glint in his eyes as he turned toward the door. She tried to follow. To be silent.

But her heart wouldn't let her.

"I'm pregnant, Antonio," she heard herself blurt out.

Pregnant?

Antonio Delacruz froze, sure he'd heard her wrong. Above them, the sky was overcast as from a distance he heard ominous thunder.

Slowly, he turned to her on the sidewalk. "What?"

"You heard me."

His eyebrows lowered fiercely. "April Fool's Day was yesterday."

"It's not a joke. I'm pregnant."

Antonio told himself he felt nothing. He wouldn't, couldn't, feel the rush of emotion suddenly circling him like a predator, looking for any crack in his armor, so it could invade and destroy his heart.

She'd slept with another man.

He tapped the roof of the car harder than necessary, and the chauffeur drove away from the curb. Forcibly relaxing his shoulders, he said merely, "I thought you had more sense."

Hana's sweep of dark eyebrows lifted over her warm brown eyes in surprise. "What?"

He wondered who the baby's father might be. She'd been a virgin when—he cut that thought off immediately. But she must have found a new lover right after.

The same week?

The same night?

For Hana, it would be easy. Any man would desire her. Unwillingly, Antonio's gaze traced over her slender form. Hana Everly was the most beautiful woman he'd ever met, though he'd spent almost two years trying to pretend she wasn't, trying to think of her as only his secretary and nothing more.

Her beauty was elusive and indefinable. All the attributes of her melting-pot American heritage combined into exquisite grace. He'd asked her once about her ancestry, and she'd shrugged. "I'm American. My family came from everywhere. England, Ireland, Brazil, Japan. Other places. And you, Mr. Delacruz?"

"Spain," he'd said shortly. It was probably true, but he'd never know for sure.

Now, Hana looked at him, her brown eyes huge in her oval face, her lips pink and full, her dark hair pulled back into a long ponytail. Always the consummate professional, she wore an elegant, feminine white skirt suit that was simple and sleek as required for the executive assistant to a billionaire, without drawing undue attention.

And yet Hana always drew attention, whether she wished it or not. Even here on the Tokyo sidewalk, as men passed by, their eyes lingered on her. She looked untouchable as a star.

But Antonio had touched her. He was the only man who ever had.

At least so he'd believed—

"Is that all you have to say to me?" Hana said in a low, harsh voice, her lovely face caught between anger and pain. "You thought I had more sense?"

"I'm disappointed," he said tightly.

"*Disappointed*," she repeated.

He'd relied on her. Believed in her. Now she was pregnant by another man. She was going to quit her job to be with him and raise their child. That had to be the reason he felt this crushing sense of emotion, like he couldn't breathe. Hana was the best damn secretary he'd ever had, and he was going to lose her.

How had she hidden her love affair from him? He and Hana had been working together day and night in Madrid and around the world, preparing to negotiate this deal. How had he not known she'd taken a lover?

Antonio had known Hana's value as his assistant. So in spite of his attraction to her, he'd never crossed the line of professionalism, not once. Not until that night in Madrid, when he'd found her crying for reasons she wouldn't explain. He'd been trying to comfort her—that was all, truly—when, like a miracle, she'd suddenly lifted up on her tiptoes and kissed him full on the lips.

That kiss…

Antonio pushed away the memory, closing down his feelings, burying them along with the other things he didn't want to remember.

All right, fine. She was leaving. He wouldn't be a jerk about it. Hana had been a good assistant. He'd try to be happy for her. After all, she'd made it all too clear she wanted the whole domestic fairy tale someday—husband, kids, house. Damn it, he'd send her off with a wedding check big enough to pay for the kid's college tuition. She'd been worth it.

He'd pay her off. He'd move on. And above all, he'd make damn sure he never let himself ask…

"Who's the father?" he heard himself say, as if his mouth was no longer controlled by his brain.

She drew back, her lovely face incredulous. "Are you kidding? You know who the father is!"

"Do I?" He frowned, searching his memory. "I'm amazed, actually. How did you manage to sneak away for an affair, in the midst of our working twenty-hour days? Does the man work for me? A gardener? A driver?"

Hana's face blazed with sudden fire. "Stop it, Antonio. Just stop."

He stared, astonished to see her so angry. Hana never showed anger. She was always patient, kind, understanding. She was the kindest person he knew. "Why are you upset?"

"Because it's you, you idiot! *You're* the father!"

Antonio's body felt the impact of the words before his mind comprehended them. He felt them like a blow. "What?"

"Of course it's you!"

Stumbling a step, he instinctively reached a hand out against the column of the building. He had to. His legs were shaking.

"Do you really think I would sleep with someone else, after we were together?" she demanded. "I can't jump in and out of affairs so quickly. Even if you can!"

If only. If only he'd been able to forget her. If only she meant nothing to him now. As the first raindrops fell from the gray sky, one fell against his cheek. Antonio stared at her, feeling sick and betrayed.

"I've been feeling out of sorts for the last month. I thought my cycle was messed up by too much work and stress and not enough sleep but…" She hesitated. "I bought a pregnancy test in Madrid. I took it on the plane, right before we landed. I'm pregnant."

When Antonio still didn't respond, Hana's forehead furrowed. Her expression became almost bewildered.

"Look," she said finally, "I know you've never been interested in anything like marriage or children. This was a surprise for me, too. We used a condom. It shouldn't have been possible. But I thought you at least had the right to—"

"Enough," he ground out. "Not another word."

"Was I wrong to tell you?" Her eyes were luminous with unshed tears that seemed utterly genuine. He despised them. And her. Most of all, he despised himself for ever letting his guard down. For thinking she was different. For believing he could trust her, as he'd trusted no one else on earth. For resisting his desire for her, day after day, so they could maintain that precious working relationship, the closest relationship of his life.

And all along, she'd been sleeping with another man. And now lying about it.

Assuming she was even pregnant at all. It was possible that, too, was a bald-faced lie.

But either way, she must have planned this all

along, from the moment she'd started working for him. She'd set him up, hoping to take a nice juicy portion of his fortune. And Hana likely would have succeeded in her goal, except for a vital fact that she didn't know.

He couldn't have gotten her pregnant. It was physically impossible.

Antonio's body shook as he reached out to take the briefcase and files from her hands. He said abruptly, "Your services are no longer required, Miss Everly."

Her luscious pink lips fell open. "You're—you're firing me?"

"You'll get severance pay as your contract dictates. But I want you gone."

"But—but why?"

"You know why."

"Because I'm pregnant with your baby?" she cried.

"Because you lied to me," he said harshly. "You tried to trap me. Tried, and failed." He narrowed his eyes. "Goodbye, Miss Everly."

Turning on his heel, Antonio went into the building, followed by his glowering bodyguard. He went through the swiveling door into the lobby where his team waited to help negotiate the Iyokan Airways deal. He left her standing alone on the sidewalk, shivering in the cold Tokyo morning. And he didn't look back.

CHAPTER TWO

SHOCKED, HANA WATCHED the father of her baby turn scornfully and leave her abandoned and alone on the Tokyo sidewalk.

Except Antonio hadn't just left her.

He'd *fired* her.

He'd taken her innocence. He'd changed her life forever. And now, to add insult to injury, he'd kicked her out of a job she loved.

Shivering, she heard another low rumble of thunder, rolling above the city, making the glass and steel and neon tremble. She felt a cool breeze against her overheated skin, and looked up at the lowering gray sky as the drizzle turned to rain.

Obviously, Hana had known that Antonio wouldn't react like the hero of a romantic movie, and kiss her joyfully at the news of her pregnancy. She'd known he didn't want children, or the slightest commitment.

But she'd never imagined he could be such an utter bastard as this.

Trembling, she wiped her eyes as she felt the cold splatter of raindrops against her face. Why was she so surprised? As his assistant, she of all people had seen how heartless Antonio Delacruz could be, especially to his lovers. She'd seen him relentlessly pursue a woman until the thrill of the conquest started to wane. It never took long—a few weeks, or perhaps even just a single night, until he was bored, finished.

Hana had always been amazed at those foolish women who let themselves care for him, each of whom apparently believed, incredibly, that she'd be the one to finally tame the untamable playboy. Hana had pitied them. Could they not see how he turned on his interest and charm like a switch? One moment, he was a passionate lover, with all the intensity of relentless desire; the next, he was gone.

Although it wasn't fair to say Antonio was just a plague to womankind. He treated everyone badly, men and women, though with men his ruthlessness was manifested by him taking their businesses if he wanted them—their businesses, and their girlfriends.

But Hana had thought she was special. For two years, she'd worked at his side, often twelve-hour days, seven days a week, and for the last few months, far more than that. She'd been inspired by him, challenged by him. His success was her success, and she'd given him every bit of her blood, sweat and tears to make CrossWorld Airways the global airline he wanted it to be.

She'd thought that they were partners of a sort, if not friends. But now she saw how truly unspecial she was.

You tried to trap me. Tried, and failed. Goodbye, Miss Everly.

The cold rain pattered the rhythm of his words against her, soaking through her dark hair and white suit. People stared at her as they passed by, all of them sensibly holding umbrellas to block the rain. She probably looked like a fool, standing there with her mouth still agape. She felt like one.

Antonio had made her one.

No, that wasn't fair. Hana took a deep breath. She'd done this to herself.

Closing her eyes, she lifted her face up to the sky. But she'd never imagined in a million years that he'd fire her for being pregnant. However the world saw him, she'd thought, at his core, Antonio Delacruz was an honorable man. She'd thought, however badly he'd treated his other mistresses, he would never act that way toward her.

Hana's eyes abruptly opened.

She, who'd always prided herself on being practical, clear-eyed and smart, had been the biggest fool of them all.

Traffic had increased on the busy street. Rain—only rain, not tears, definitely not tears—made her vision blurry as she looked down at her white suit, now plastered to her skin, gray as a dove in the wan light.

She'd devoted her life to him, been honest with him in spite of her fear, and this was how he repaid her?

He'd insulted her. He'd fired her. And worst of all: he'd coldly rejected his own child, now growing inside her.

A white-hot flame of anger burned through her. It grew inside Hana, grew and grew until it left room for nothing else in her heart.

She and the baby were on their own.

Hana lifted her chin. Fine. They didn't need him. They'd be better off without him—soulless, heartless, backstabbing jerk!

Her hands tightened on the strap of her purse. Her satchel of clothes was unfortunately still in the back of the Rolls-Royce that had brought them from Haneda Airport. All she had in the small black purse over her shoulder was her passport, credit cards and a little bit of cash, a mix of yen, dollars and euros. But she was also in Tokyo, which meant she had something more.

Ren.

Her best friend, whom she saw just a few times a year. Just thinking of his kindly face made her want to get to him as quickly as possible.

Blinking back hot, furious tears, she waved down a taxi. As one started to pull to the curb, she saw the driver hesitate, looking at her in the rain, obviously fearing she'd flood his upholstery given half a chance. But then he sighed and pulled his taxi over.

"Sumimasen," she said over the lump in her throat, trying very hard to keep the wettest parts of her clothing off the seat. Holding her bag tightly against her chest, she gave him the address in Harajuku then stared out at the passing streets. Ren Tanaka. It was by sheerest luck that she'd had her heart broken in the same city where her best friend lived.

She and Ren had been friends since childhood, when they'd been pen pals as Hana traveled the world with her adventurous teacher parents. He was the only friend she'd kept in touch with,

moving as often as she did, first with her restless parents and then later, working for an airline tycoon. Hana was an only child, an orphan
now that her parents and grandparents had died,
but somehow, in their frequent online conversations, Ren had become her family.

Although...

Unease went through her as she remembered
the last time she'd seen him, on a brief business
trip to Tokyo a few months earlier. He'd acted
very strangely. It wasn't actually what he'd said,
so much as the way he'd looked at her. It had
made her nervous.

Was it possible that somehow, after all their
years of friendship, Ren could have gotten some
crazy idea that he was in love with her?

Absolutely not, Hana told herself. Why would
Ren imagine himself in love with her, when he
had so many girls interested in him, right here
in Tokyo?

He was her dear friend, like always. And he'd
help her figure out what to do now. Hana tried
to imagine what he'd say when he heard about
her unexpected pregnancy—and how her boss
had abandoned and fired her. Ren already disliked Antonio intensely, though the two men had
never actually met. Her boss didn't even know

of Ren's existence. Why would he? Hana's child-hood friendship had been entirely through letters, and even now it was mostly online.

As the taxi turned toward the hip, colorful street in Harajuku where Ren managed his family's boutique hotel, she took a deep breath. She was not going to cry over Antonio. No way, no how. He wasn't worth it. He'd proven himself totally unworthy of either Hana or their baby.

So she'd move on. Think only of the future. She'd put Antonio Delacruz behind her and never, ever think of him again.

But still, she heard the echo of Antonio's sensual voice spoken into the hot, dark Spanish night.

There will be no romance, no marriage. No consequences.

And in spite of her resolve to feel nothing, Hana gasped out a sob, hating him with fresh, hot tears.

Liar!

"Possible?" Antonio choked out, dumbfounded. "What do you mean, it's possible?"

"Just what I said." The doctor looked at him gravely over his thick glasses. "We did the test, as you requested. And the results are conclusive."

It was good Antonio was already sitting down. He felt sick and dizzy at the news. The minimalist decor and medical equipment in the examining room of the private clinic swam in front of his eyes.

"I don't understand," he stammered. "As I told you, I had a vasectomy eighteen years ago, at a reputable hospital—"

"Yes. It seems your body has healed itself."

Antonio stared at the doctor in shock.

All morning, he'd felt his insides churn, in spite of his best efforts not to think about the lies Hana had told him on the sidewalk: pretending to be pregnant with his baby, clearly in an attempt to extort money or a proposal of marriage. Going to the top floor of the skyscraper with his team, he'd pushed aside the feelings of betrayal and rage, and tried to focus on the details of the business negotiation.

But the meeting had been a disaster. He hadn't been able to find the right papers in the portfolio, or track down the points he'd previously marked to discuss with his lawyers before they formally presented the offer to Iyokan Airways. Hana had always been in charge of solving his problems, finding papers, sorting out details, arranging whatever he needed.

Now he was alone.

Abandoned.

Betrayed.

During the meeting, his lawyers and his Tokyo lead team had looked at each other worriedly as they were forced to repeat certain clauses in the contract multiple times to their normally razor-sharp boss. Emotion—rage and anger and, worst of all, hurt—had built inside him, until finally, it had exploded. He'd scattered the pile of papers in fury across the large glass table in his conference room on the top floor of the skyscraper, with its view of Tokyo.

"Reschedule," he'd growled, and stalked out, knowing they were probably wondering if he was drunk, or if he'd lost his mind—or his nerve. His business rivals would smell blood in the water. He himself had always enjoyed attacking the businesses of weaker opponents. He'd never experienced what it was like to be on the other side of it. Not since he was young, when he was helpless and alone—

He pushed the memory aside. This was Hana's fault. His secretary had betrayed him at every level. Personally. Professionally.

He never should have slept with her. The success of his company was far more important than any sexual desire. CrossWorld Airways was the only thing that mattered. Once he expanded routes into Asia, he would build to Africa and South America. He would have the first truly global low-cost airline. His company was his family, his lover, his religion and meaning. His company was his soul.

So why had he done it? Why, when she'd kissed him, that night in Madrid, hadn't he had the strength to push her away?

Yes, Hana was beautiful. But he'd ignored beautiful women before. It was something more. She'd been different. Pure fire. And when she'd kissed him, he could have no more pushed her away then he could have stopped breathing.

He'd wanted her then. He wanted her still.

But she'd been setting a trap for him, all along. Playing him for a fool, luring him in with her innocent beauty and apparent warm heart. All so she could seduce him and claim to be pregnant. He could hardly believe he'd been tricked so thoroughly.

But that was the problem.

The whole thing was hard to believe.

And the more Antonio had thought about it during the business meeting, the more distracted he'd become, obsessing over a single question.

How was it possible everything about Hana was a lie?

For two years, she'd worked at his side. She'd been hardworking, loyal, honest to a fault. How could anyone maintain an act like that so well, and for so long?

Antonio couldn't understand it. And every time he'd tried to focus during the business meeting, he'd seen the eviscerated look in her eyes. *You're firing me? Because I'm pregnant with your baby?*

And he'd felt his heart, his guts, every part of his body twist like a rag wrung dry.

Stalking angrily from the meeting, he'd grimly arranged to see the best fertility doctor in the city. Just to prove, once and for all, that Hana Everly was a liar. He hadn't done anything wrong. He was the victim here.

And now this.

He'd come to the clinic for reassurance, not to discover his worst fears were actually true. He'd never expected he'd be told it was possible that he'd fathered Hana's child!

"No," Antonio told the doctor hoarsely. "I had a vasectomy!"

The other man stroked his white beard thoughtfully. "You had the procedure when you were very young. Sometimes the body heals itself, as I said. It's rare, less than one percent of cases. But it happens." He paused. "We can book an appointment to redo the procedure…"

"What's the point of that now? It's already too late!" With a low snarl, Antonio rose to his feet and stormed out of the clinic. All he could think about was the stricken look on Hana's face when he'd left her standing alone on the sidewalk. The shock in her brown eyes.

If she was really pregnant with his child, and he'd treated her like that—

Antonio pushed the thought away ruthlessly. It wasn't his fault. How could he have possibly known the vasectomy he'd had as a teenager would fail nearly two decades later? Of course he'd assumed Hana was lying. How could he think otherwise? People had always proved themselves worthy of his worst assumptions.

Everyone except Hana. But he'd been all too ready to believe the worst even of her. Because it scared him, how much he'd come to trust her.

As he stepped out of the medical clinic, Antonio saw the rain had lightened to a drizzle, with flashes of sunlight like silver breaking through the clouds.

You're firing me? Because I'm pregnant with your baby?

He felt another twist in his gut.

"Mr. Delacruz, if I may speak freely..." His longtime bodyguard Ramon Garcia, who'd been waiting in the lobby, followed him toward the waiting car. "*Señor*, I think you've made a mistake about Miss Everly. She's a good person. She didn't deserve to be treated like that."

Perfecto. This was just what he needed. One more person judging him. And now that Antonio knew he was indeed in the wrong, he *really* didn't want to hear it. "It's none of your business, Garcia."

The man's accusing eyes met his. "If you didn't intend to step up, you never should have slept with her—"

"Enough," he snapped, causing his bodyguard's jaw to set. Wonderful, another trusted employee enraged with him. Antonio's shoulders were tight as he climbed into the waiting Rolls-Royce. Garcia got into the front seat without a word.

"Where to, sir?" the driver asked him after a pause.

"Just drive," Antonio ground out.

Looking out at the soft drizzle in the spring

afternoon, his eyes fell on the pink cherry trees. Hana had been so excited that the negotiations would be in Tokyo at the same time the trees were likely to bloom. *They bloom for such a short time,* she'd said. *It's precious and beautiful. You have to enjoy it while you can. Before it's gone.*

Just like their night together, he thought.

For years, almost from the day he'd hired her, he'd resisted seducing her only by an act of pure will, because of her importance to his company.

Then she'd kissed him, and all his self-control had exploded to dust, burned away by fire. For the first time in his adult life, he'd given in to the demands of his body, the demands of his heart, over the cold decision of his reason.

Antonio had tried to tell himself that bedding her could somehow be a good thing for their working relationship. That it could end his desire for her. He'd even extracted a promise from Hana that they'd both forget the night ever happened—a promise he knew he himself could not fulfill.

Useless, all useless. From the morning he'd woken up with her soft naked body in his arms, he'd discovered taking her virginity hadn't lessened his desire, only increased it. His need for her had been a constant torment for the next two months as they'd worked together round the clock on the Iyokan Airways deal. Every time he'd felt her brush against him innocently as they looked over documents together, he'd grasp the desk, remembering how he'd held her virgin body naked against his in the breathless heat of passion. As he heard her speak of business details, he'd hear, against his will, her cry as she'd gasped out with pleasure, gripping his back so tightly, he could still feel the marks of her fingernails—not against his skin, but against his heart.

It had terrified him.

Antonio had known, if he ever touched her again, it would destroy everything he cared about. His company would be hurt by her loss, and he would certainly lose her. Their working relationship could perhaps survive a one-night stand, but not a full-blown affair. He never kept a mistress for long. And how many times had Hana told him that her biggest dream was to someday have a real home, commitment, marriage, children? All things he could never give, not to her or anyone.

So he'd done the impossible. He'd pretended

their night together had been forgettable. That it had, in fact, already been forgotten by him.

He'd been the one lying all this time. Not Hana.

Staring out the window blankly as his chauffeur drove him through Tokyo, Antonio looked down and realized his phone was somehow in his hands. Without letting himself think, he dialed Hana's number.

She didn't answer.

He tried again.

Same result.

No wonder, he thought grimly. He'd fired her, hadn't he? She was no longer obligated to pick up when he called.

"Find her," he barked at his bodyguard.

Turning in the front seat, Garcia's rough face lifted into a crooked smile. "Her best friend lives in Tokyo. If she's not answering the phone, she's probably with him."

"Who is he?" he demanded in a strained voice.

"His name is Ren Tanaka. His family owns a hotel in Harajuku."

A best friend? A man? Antonio didn't know which surprised him more. But as his driver changed route through the crowded streets, he told himself he wasn't jealous, just curious.

Hana had been a virgin; of that, there could be no doubt. And it wasn't like Antonio had any claim on her.

Except that she was expecting his baby.

A baby.

After everything Antonio had done to prevent fatherhood, he was going to have a child.

A lump rose to his throat as he looked out at the passing streets of Tokyo in the soft spring mist.

Hana would be better off raising the child without him, obviously. What did he know of fatherhood? He'd never had parents. Better to stick with the choices he'd made long ago—to focus on his company and his fortune. They were the only things that mattered.

He'd gotten a vasectomy for a reason. He didn't have the capacity to commit to anyone for life. He wasn't fit to be a husband or father. Hana wouldn't be shocked by this. She knew him better than anyone. All he could offer was financial support. It shouldn't be hard for him to convince her.

As long as he didn't touch her. Damn it, he was only a man. If he touched her, he would take her. Not just for a one-night stand. His re-pressed desire for her had become a ferocious beast, which if unleashed, would be unstoppable. He'd keep her as his mistress until his body was utterly satiated, whether that took days, weeks, or even months. For Antonio, sex was a physical thing, like eating or sleeping. But Hana's heart was warm, not frozen like his own. All those months in his bed might lure her into blindly loving him. Then, when their affair inevitably ended, her love would just as inevitably turn to hate.

And perhaps she'd teach the baby to hate him as well...

No. He could never touch Hana again.

"We're here, *señor.*"

Getting out of car, Antonio remembered Hana's satchel in the trunk and got it out. He felt new shame as he remembered how he'd fired her, sending her off without even her bag of clothes. As he lifted it to his shoulder, a crack of sunlight burst through the clouds. Harajuku was very different from the financial district, crowded, lively and colorful. He looked up at the seven-story hotel silhouetted against the soft gray sky. Garcia started to follow, until he gestured sharply for his bodyguard to stay. He wanted to talk to Hana alone.

The last thing he wanted to do was hurt her,

or the baby. But he was a selfish bastard, and that wasn't going to change.

And Hana would be an amazing mother. The baby would never even miss having him as a father. After all, what did Antonio have to offer a child, beyond his fortune? There was no question of Antonio being more involved than that. He'd give Hana an enormous financial settlement. They'd be set for life.

Now all he had to do was convince her of that.

Walking through the sleekly modern Japanese-style lobby of the hotel, he stopped a passing employee.

"Sir?" the man responded politely.

"Is an American girl staying here? A guest of Ren Tanaka?"

The employee looked Antonio over from his bespoke suit to his Italian leather shoes, then with a nod, motioned toward a quiet, darkened bar, separate from the lobby. "They're in there."

Glancing at the door, he set his jaw. Then he held out the satchel. "Make sure this is delivered to her room."

"Of course, sir."

Leaving the lobby, Antonio stood for a moment in the doorway of the darkened hotel bar.

It took several seconds for his eyes to adjust. He blinked. Then blinked again.

Then he sucked in his breath when he saw Hana sitting alone at a table, across the empty bar. Her white skirt suit was edged with a sultry blue glow from the neon light on the ceiling. His body was instantly electrified. "Hana."

Turning, she saw him. "Antonio?" She rose unsteadily to her feet. "What are you doing here?"

"I had to see you," he said, searching her beautiful face.

She glanced uneasily at something on the other side of the bar. "Why?"

"I…uh…" Now that he was looking at her, all his carefully planned arguments flew from his mind. Against his will, his gaze fell to her trembling, deliciously full pink lips, and down farther still. Her breasts seemed bigger—yes—the top two buttons of her white fitted jacket were stretched about to burst. How had he not noticed that before today?

Because he hadn't wanted to notice.

But he wanted her. Suddenly. Savagely. So much his hands shook with it. He wanted to grab her, push her back against the wall. He didn't care what the cost might be to his company, to his peace of mind, to anything. He wanted to have her even if the cost was setting fire to the world.

"Delacruz. It's you, isn't it?"

Hearing a man's low growl, Antonio turned and saw a young Japanese man, tall and handsome in a sleek suit, perhaps ten years younger than Antonio's thirty-six years, approaching from behind the bar.

"Who are you?" he asked, though he'd already guessed.

The man's lip curled. "My name is Ren Tanaka."

Antonio's eyes narrowed as he sized up the younger man. "So you're her *best friend*."

He lifted his chin. "And you're her bastard boss who got her pregnant and abandoned her like a—"

He spoke a Japanese word that Antonio didn't understand, but the meaning was plain enough. Tanaka looked as if he'd like to strangle him with his bare hands.

The feeling was mutual. As Antonio saw the other man gently hand Hana a glass of water, then step protectively in front of her—as if he were trying to protect her from Antonio!—his own hands clenched into fists.

Then he saw Hana's face, her worry and fear as she looked between the two men. He saw the way her body, newly lush with his child, was trembling.

With almost superhuman restraint, Antonio forced his hands to relax. He'd already shown her enough bad behavior today. And he didn't give a damn about Tanaka. That wasn't why he'd come.

"Can we go and talk?" he asked Hana in a low voice.

"You don't have to go anywhere with him," Tanaka said to her. Setting his jaw, he scowled at Antonio. "Leave my hotel. You are not welcome here."

His eyes narrowed. "You'd do well to stay out of this, *friend*."

"You've hurt Hana enough. I'm not going to give you another chance."

"Why?" Antonio lifted his lip in a snarl. "You want her for yourself?"

The younger man lifted his chin. "What if I do?"

"Back off, or I'll knock you flat into the wall."

"I'd like to see you try."

"No!" Hana pushed anxiously between them, separating them before either could throw the first punch. She looked at them pleadingly. "No, please—don't!"

The two men glared at each other. Antonio itched to shove the other man aside. He was shocked by his own rage. He'd never felt so possessive about any woman before.

But Hana was different. And Antonio suddenly knew, with stunning clarity, that he'd never let Ren Tanaka—or any other man on earth—have her.

Because Hana Everly was his.

CHAPTER THREE

How HAD THINGS spiraled so far out of control, so fast?

"Stop it! Both of you!" Hana cried. "This isn't helping anything!"

"It would help if I punched his smug face," Ren muttered in Japanese.

Glancing swiftly at Antonio, she saw that even though he didn't speak the language, he'd understood Ren's meaning perfectly. He narrowed his dark eyes.

The last few hours had been exhausting. Going from that ghastly scene with Antonio on the sidewalk to coming here to talk to Ren had been a classic case of frying pan to fire. She'd never forget the look on Ren's face when she'd told him she was pregnant by her boss.

"I knew it," Ren had breathed, then his eyes had flashed fire. "I'm going to kill him."

It hadn't been easy to talk him out of immediately going to find Antonio and start a fight.

It was almost funny. Hana had come here looking for comfort. But instead, she'd spent the last few hours trying to make *Ren* feel better.

"Are you sure?" he'd kept asking incredulously. "Are you really sure you're pregnant?"

To shut him up, she'd finally let him take her to the hotel's on-call doctor, who had an office down the street. They'd just barely returned from the appointment, where Hana had learned what she already knew: she was two and a half months pregnant.

But she'd heard the baby's heartbeat for the first time, which had been wondrous to her. And bittersweet. She'd kept thinking of her baby's father, and thinking Antonio should have been there, then remembering with fresh pain how he'd rejected them both.

Ren didn't exactly offer much solace. All the way back from the clinic, Ren had demanded over and over, "And you told Delacruz? But he abandoned you? He denied being the father? Then he *fired* you?"

None of it was very comforting.

Just a few minutes earlier, as they returned to his family's small hotel where he was manager, Ren had growled again that he was going to go look for Delacruz and make him regret treating her so badly. To distract him, Hana had asked for a glass of water, and a quiet place to sit down and catch her breath. He'd immediately become solicitous and led her to the darkened, empty bar while he went to fetch her water.

Then, like some apparition of a demon brought by the speaking of his name, Antonio himself had appeared in the doorway.

Now, the two men were bristling like full-grown stags ready to clash at each other with sharp, murderous antlers.

"Stay out of this, Tanaka." Then Antonio turned to her, and his voice became gentle. "Can we go somewhere to talk, Hana?"

"What more could you possibly say to me?" she said, at the same time Ren snarled, "She doesn't want to talk to you!"

"Please," Antonio said, looking only at her. She took a deep breath.

"Fine." She put a restraining hand on her friend's sleeve. "It's all right. I'll talk to him."

Ren's face was a glower. "He doesn't deserve it."

Hana gave a rueful smile. "He's my baby's father. I have to hear him out." She turned to Antonio. "Here?"

Antonio shook his head. He started to reach

his hand toward her, then abruptly stopped himself. Turning away without touching her, he said gruffly, "Follow me."

Outside the hotel, the sky had turned blue and the sun was shining, in the bright changeability of early April.

But that was nothing compared to the unpredictability of her baby's father, Hana thought. As they stood in the small, crowded street, filled with pastel-colored shops, outrageously dressed mannequins, toy shops, fashionable high schoolers, so vibrant and young, Hana looked up at Antonio's darkly handsome face.

"All right, we're alone. What do you want?"

"Not yet," he said grimly, glancing behind them. Following his gaze, she saw Ren's face watching from the hotel lobby. A group of laughing girls walked by, wearing bold clothes and makeup, their eyes lingering on Antonio's handsome face and powerful frame. He said grimly, "Let's go where it's not so crowded."

Hana followed him down the small street to a larger avenue. Passing Harajuku Station, they crossed a bridge into a large, beautiful park. They walked some distance in silence, through a forest, past an impressive shrine.

Hana took a deep breath of the cool, fragrant

air, feeling the dappled warmth of the spring sun on her face, beneath the pink-and-white flowering cherry trees. She realized she was trembling as she waited for him to speak. Why? What more could Antonio possibly say to hurt her?

Nothing. Whatever it was, she told herself she wouldn't care.

Finally stopping in a quiet clearing, he turned to face her. "What did you tell Tanaka about me?"

"The truth," she said.

Antonio tilted his head. His black eyes were glinting in the sun, the hard line of his jaw already growing dark with five o'clock shadow. "That I was a heartless monster who seduced you, got you pregnant and then abandoned you?"

"I didn't tell him you seduced me." She set her jaw. "Is that why you tracked me across Tokyo? To give me a hard time for sobbing on a friend's shoulder?"

His dark eyes flashed. *"Friend?"* he repeated incredulously. "The man's in love with you!"

She could hardly deny it, not when Ren had acted like she was his personal property. She looked away. "I... I don't know what that's all about. We've been friends since childhood."

"Is he your lover?"

Hana glared at him. "Don't be ridiculous! He's like a brother to me!"

"He wasn't looking at you like a brother."

Was that jealousy she heard in Antonio's voice? No—impossible. He never cared enough about any woman to be jealous. She lifted her chin. "Why do you care?"

"I don't."

She felt an ache in her throat. "If you only came to yell at me, then I'm going back..."

But as she turned, he stopped her with his husky voice.

"Wait. Please."

"Wait for what?" She lifted her chin. "For you to find new ways to insult me and hurt me? I've had enough of that."

"No. Damn it." He clawed his hand through his dark, rumpled hair. "I'm doing this all wrong. I came..." Taking a deep breath, Antonio came closer. "I came to tell you I'm sorry."

Hana's jaw dropped. In two years of working for him, she'd never heard him apologize to anyone. For anything.

"*Sorry,*" she repeated numbly.

"Yes." He came closer, not touching her. "Please. You have to let me explain."

Antonio Delacruz, who never explained himself to anyone, wanted to explain to her? Her mouth was dry as she said, "Go ahead."

He stood in front of her, starkly handsome and broad-shouldered in his sleek black suit and long coat. Behind him, the park was a kaleidoscope of color, green and pink and white, beneath the sun's golden light and bright blue sky.

His black eyes seemed strangely vulnerable, in a way she'd never seen before. "This isn't easy."

"Good," she said, refusing to show him any mercy.

"I treated you badly," he acknowledged.

"Badly?"

He gave a crooked smile. "Really badly."

"It took all of my courage to tell you I was pregnant. I know how you are. I knew you wouldn't exactly be overjoyed at the news. But I never thought you'd accuse me of lying to you!" She shook her head fiercely. "Even with a condom, you know sex always comes with some risk of pregnancy, you know that, right? Plus, you know *me*! How could you do that?"

Antonio looked down at her. "I had a vasectomy, Hana. Eighteen years ago."

In the distance, she could see the tips of modern buildings gleaming over the park, against the vivid blue sky. "Wh-what?"

"It's true."

"You were just a teenager then!"

"Barely eighteen."

"But why—why would you do something so permanent to yourself? How could you?"

Setting his jaw, he shook his head. "Why I did it doesn't matter. Not anymore." He gave a sudden snort. "And as it turned out, it wasn't so permanent."

"What do you mean?"

"After you told me you were pregnant, I couldn't think about anything else. So I canceled the business meeting—"

"You did what?"

"And I went to a doctor, where I was told that, somehow, my body had healed itself. It's rare, the doctor said. The rate is less than one percent. But it happens. And it happened to me."

She was staring at him openmouthed. "You canceled the meeting?"

He gave a wry smile. "*That's* the thing that surprises you?"

"You've been working like a madman for months—"

"I had to. I thought I knew you. How could you be a lying gold digger, trying to lure me into bed and trick me into marriage?"

"I wasn't!" she said indignantly.

"But there was no other explanation, don't you see? I'd had a vasectomy. I couldn't be the father of your baby. You couldn't possibly be telling me the truth." He paused. "I went to a private clinic so I could prove, once and for all, that you were lying." He gave her a rueful smile. "But it turned out that I was the one who was wrong. And you were right."

A soft breeze stroked the blossoms lazily, and ruffled his dark hair against his forehead. She fought the sudden impulse to brush it back with her fingertips.

Tightening her hands at her sides, Hana looked past him, to the families with blankets spread out beneath the flowering trees, enjoying a late lunch in the festive tradition of *hanami*. She looked at the nearest family, a smiling young couple with a toddler, picnicking together on a blanket.

"I was wrong to accuse you of lying," Antonio said, bowing his head. "I'm sorry. I won't insult you by asking for a paternity test. I know the baby's mine."

She looked at him. "Just like that?"

"Just like that."

For a moment, their eyes locked, and she felt the electricity of his gaze go straight to her heart.

Then his jaw tightened, and he looked away. "But you and I both know I'd be no good at raising a baby."

The lump returned to her throat. "Yes. I know."

"You aren't going to argue?"

She gave him a wistful smile. "I know you, Antonio. Of course you don't want to raise a baby. I only told you about the pregnancy because it was the right thing to do. But I know you're not interested in becoming a husband or father."

"Oh." He blinked, then continued awkwardly, "I will of course pay child support. And give you a large settlement to provide for the baby—"

"I don't want your money." It was exactly what she'd expected, so why did she feel hurt? Of course he'd offer her money for her baby. What else could he give? His time? His love? She said thickly, "We'll be fine."

He frowned. "But of course you will have a settlement. You deserve it. You earned it."

"Earned it how?" Her pride suddenly flared. "On my back in your bed?"

He scowled at her. "I didn't mean it that way—"

"I know," she cut him off. She'd been rude. But her heart was aching as she thought how different it should have been, sharing the joy of her pregnancy news. How happy and sweet today would have been, if she'd just taken her grandmother's advice and waited for marriage! If she'd waited until she'd found her true partner and home!

Swallowing, she looked across the beautiful cherry tree blooms against the wide blue sky. "You've paid me a very good salary, and I've saved most of it for the past year. Working and traveling so much, I had no time to spend it." She lifted her chin. "*That* is what I've earned. And until I get a new job, the baby and I will be fine."

"Hana, you're being unreasonable."

"It's my choice. I don't want your payoff money."

"It's not a payoff."

"Of course it is."

He ground his teeth. "What is it you want, Hana? Marriage? We both know that's not going to happen."

A low, bitter laugh came unbidden from her throat. "You think I want to marry you?" She shook her head. "It must be amazing to be you,

Antonio, always confident that you're the center of the world."

"Come on, Hana. You've spent two years at my side. You know how I am."

Yes, she did. She remembered all the women who'd tried so desperately to marry him over the last two years. How sorry she'd felt for them. She'd always been attracted to her boss, but she'd heeded the warnings. She would never love him. Her own parents' intense, almost teenager-like relationship had soured her on the idea of romantic love anyway.

Besides, it was bad enough that, as his employee, she'd based the last two years of her life entirely around Antonio's needs. She'd traveled when he traveled, lived where he lived, worked when he worked. The opposite of the life she actually wanted.

Since her rootless childhood, Hana had yearned for a real home. But when her beloved grandmother had become sick, Hana had dropped out of college. Desperate to provide Sachiko with the comfort and care of the best medical facility, she'd gotten a job. Giving up her own dreams, she'd taken increasingly demanding, high-paying secretarial jobs requiring her to travel constantly around the world.

Her grandmother had died a year ago. Hana could have quit her job then. But she hadn't.

Because as challenging as it was to work for Antonio, she'd come to love it. Somehow, his house in Madrid had become like home.

It shouldn't have felt that way. With all their traveling, they only lived there part-time. And though she'd become friends with the house staff, the palace still wasn't exactly homey, but ridiculously big with a ballroom and vast echoing hallways.

And yet, two months ago, when Antonio announced out of the blue he was going to sell the Madrid house and move the company's headquarters to New York, she'd felt a pain in her heart she hadn't expected. "Time to move on," he'd told her casually as he looked around the home office where they'd spent untold hours together. He'd shrugged. "There's nothing I care about in Madrid anymore."

A few hours later, he'd been astonished to find her crying in the *palacio*'s hallway. Shocked, he'd demanded to know the reason. But how could Hana explain, when she didn't understand it herself?

She had no claim on his house in Madrid. Just as she had no claim on Antonio.

It was time for her to go, she'd realized. To quit her job and move on, so she could finally find a home that no one could ever take from her.

But even as she'd had the thought, she'd suddenly lifted up on her tiptoes and kissed him. With an intake of breath, he'd stared at her. Then he'd grabbed her and kissed her back with passionate need.

Leading to her pregnancy now.

She never should have let herself trade their professional relationship for a personal one. Their argument this morning notwithstanding, Antonio had always treated Hana with respect far greater than he gave his mistresses. If anything, he seemed to enjoy treating his girlfriends badly. Almost as if he *wanted* them to leave him as soon as possible.

She'd felt such great pity for his last mistress, a beautiful Instagram fitness model who'd clung to him in the face of all his rudeness, that Hana had actually arranged a Christmas gift for the girl, a rare vintage camera. She'd signed Antonio's name to the card. As his secretary, Hana figured it was her job to try to make it at least *appear* that Antonio had normal human feelings—her job to make him look good, or at least less bad.

But it had been useless. Antonio had been furious at her interference, and he'd broken up with his mistress anyway. On Christmas morning, too. Well, at least the girl still had the camera as a parting gift.

Hana looked at him now beneath the cherry trees.

"You're right," she said in a low voice. "I do know you. It's probably for the best you don't want to be part of our baby's life. You'd be a horrible father, and we both know it. And as a husband—" She rolled her eyes heavenward, as if there were no words.

For a moment, Antonio's face was shocked. Then he looked inexplicably offended. "*Horrible* seems rather a strong word—"

She held up her hand to stave off his protest. "I'm just agreeing with you. You're incapable of being a father. You have absolutely nothing to offer us except money. And since I don't need that, there's nothing more to discuss, is there?"

Antonio opened his mouth. Closed it. Finally, he said tightly, "I apologized. Why are you still attacking me?"

"Attacking? You should be glad!"

He ground his teeth. "Glad you're telling me

I'd be a poor excuse for a father and an even worse husband?"

"Glad I'm not trying to change you!" She shook her head. "You can move on with your life, Antonio. Get your air routes into Asia. Expand the company worldwide, gather more billions into your bank account. I won't bother you." She lifted her chin. "You won't be my baby's father, you're no longer my boss. You're not my lover, nor even my friend. So I think we can agree there's no reason for us to ever see each other again." She stuck out her hand. "Goodbye, Antonio."

He looked down at it. She felt the sizzle from his gaze, and suddenly realized her mistake. She tried to pull her hand back, but it was too late.

Antonio took her hand in his larger one.

Just that simple contact, palm to palm, caused her to gasp. Electricity sizzled through her, from her scalp to her toes.

His expression changed, and his hand tightened on hers.

"I can't let you go," he said quietly.

"You can't?" she breathed.

"Maybe I won't be a good father. Maybe I can't be a husband. But I still don't want to let you go." Antonio pulled her closer, searching her gaze intently. "Stay with me, Hana. As my mistress."

"Mistress?" The word was slippery on her tongue, causing a flood of desire to pulse through her blood, tightening her nipples as tension coiled low and deep inside her. *Mistress.* "For how long?"

He gave her a sensual smile, lifting his other hand to her cheek. "As long as we want."

Barely able to breathe, Hana stared up at his handsome face, his dark eyes, his sculpted cheekbones, the five o'clock shadow on his hard jawline. His cruel mouth.

As long as we want.

He meant as long as *he* wanted, she realized. A month. A week. Even a night. She'd seen it play out, time and time again. Hadn't she just been pitying those foolish women who fell for him, just seconds before?

And yet she'd never expected to be asked. Not like this. It felt strangely difficult to refuse, with his dark eyes burning through her as the memory of their night together pounded through her blood.

"And the baby?" she said hoarsely.

Antonio shrugged. "We'll see. Maybe I could be some kind of father to it. Who knows?"

Maybe? A father to *it*?

A shudder went through her. *Maybe* had nothing to do with her idea of family. Family was forever. Family was all a person had to cling to in a chaotic, uncertain world.

What he was talking about was something else entirely. He was a petulant boy, not wanting to be parted from a toy.

Hana ripped herself away from the temptation of his touch. "You can't just amuse yourself for a while and then toss us aside when you're bored. I won't let you do it. Not to me and definitely not to the baby!"

He stared at her incredulously. "Don't you understand, Hana? I'm offering to let you live with me. That's more than I've ever offered any woman."

Antonio actually believed he was offering her something precious. She saw that in his handsome face. He expected her to squeal with delight, throw her arms around him and scream *"Yes!"*

He was inviting her to live with him, but he didn't seem to realize she'd already done that for two years, living at his beck and call.

The only difference was that now she'd also service him in bed. She'd live with him as his girlfriend, at his whim and on his schedule, grateful for any time and attention he chose to give her or their child, assuming their relationship even lasted until the baby was born. And when Antonio chose to leave, she'd be expected to let him go without complaint. She wouldn't even have the dignity or security she'd had as his secretary.

That was the deal he offered her. He'd possibly be a father to their child, or possibly not; he wasn't willing to commit, but still, either way, she was supposed to be grateful, and put her heart on the hook to twist whichever way his wind blew.

Her body reacted before her brain, snapping her spine straight. Anger washed through her like a flash flood, knocking out every other emotion as she looked up at him in cold fury.

"No," she said flatly.

No? *No?*

Antonio stared at her in shock, hardly able to believe he'd heard her right.

No?

He couldn't remember the last time he'd heard the word *no*, from anyone, for any reason. Hearing it from a lover was particularly shocking, especially after he'd fought for the last hour to resist his need to possess her, and stick to his original plan.

He'd never expected, if he surrendered to his overwhelming desire for her—even offering to give up his precious freedom and allow her to live with him, in his house—that she might refuse.

Antonio glared at her, feeling somehow betrayed, as if she'd lured him into this moment, just so she could reject and humiliate him.

"Why?" he demanded. How could she say no? She wanted him as much as he wanted her. *Didn't she?*

Hana raised her chin. "I went to see a doctor this morning, too." She looked down at her waistline beneath her white skirt suit. "I heard our baby's heartbeat."

The baby's heartbeat. What a strange idea. "And?"

With a slight smile, she put her hand on her belly. "Everything is coming along just fine," she said softly. "I'm due in mid-October."

Beneath the warm sun in the Tokyo park, his gaze followed hers. The barest curve beneath her white fitted jacket hinted at the child growing inside her. A baby. His baby. Setting his jaw, he pushed all emotion away. "Another reason for you to live with me."

She narrowed her lovely brown eyes. "I don't want my baby to be part of your world. Whatever made you become like this…"

"Like what?"

"So cold, so distant, so untrusting." Hana took a deep breath, then added, "So broken."

Broken? Anger shot through him. He said tightly, "You don't know me. You don't know anything about me."

"Don't I?" Hana gave him a wistful smile as the sun went behind a passing cloud. "I know you don't want a family and won't commit to anyone, ever. Why would I want to raise my child with a man like that? Even if I thought you'd actually stick around. Which I don't."

His lips parted. He wanted to defy her words, to tell her that he could commit anytime he wanted, he simply chose not to. But the words dried up in his mouth.

Her expression changed as she watched him. She shook her head, looking yearningly toward the happy young family picnicking nearby beneath the blooming cherry trees. "My parents were teachers and we moved to a new country each year. I was rarely in one place long enough to make friends. Growing up, family was all I had."

"I find that hard to imagine." Antonio remembered her grandmother's funeral last year, when so many people had come forward to comfort Hana. "You seem to make friends wherever you go." His lips suddenly tightened. "Like Ren Tanaka."

"He's my oldest friend," she said softly. "Almost like family."

"How is it that I never knew of his existence?"

She lifted her eyes. "Because you don't pay attention to anyone's life but your own."

"That's not true."

She gave a humorless smile. "I know you, Antonio."

"You don't know everything," he said tightly. No one knew about his childhood—he'd made sure of that. He himself had tried to forget how he'd been shown, over and over, that he hadn't been wanted as a child, not by anyone. Twice, foster families had brought him home from the orphanage. Twice, he'd been sent right back. The final time, when he was six years old, it had been because his foster mother had unexpectedly become pregnant. "Nothing personal, boy," his foster father had explained kindly. "But we're having our own baby now, so we don't need you anymore."

Broken.

Yes. Hana was right. She did know him. She'd seen the dark truth in his soul that he'd spent his life trying to hide. The secret no one else knew about Antonio Delacruz, playboy airline billionaire: there was some huge flaw in his soul. Something monstrous about him that had made his birth parents decide to abandon him when he was just hours old, leaving their nameless newborn in a basket on the steps of a Spanish church in the middle of the night.

"What happened to you?" Hana asked gently, drawing closer. "Why would you have a vasectomy when you were only eighteen? How could you already know you never wanted to be a father?"

Her questions felt like stabs through his heart. He couldn't let her see through his armor to the weakness beneath. He couldn't. Not anyone. But especially not her.

She was getting too close. Fortunately, he knew exactly how to push people away—by attacking their weaknesses, to distract them from seeing his.

Stepping back from her as the soft cherry petals whirled around them in the park, he said in a bored voice, "Why did I get a vasectomy? Because I'm a selfish bastard, obviously. Which as you said, you know better than anyone. Which begs the question." His eyes pierced hers. "Why did you kiss me that night?"

Hana's cheeks darkened to deep pink as she looked away. She mumbled something.

"What?"

Looking at her feet, she said, "When you told me you were going to sell the house in Madrid," her voice became stilted, "it made me sad."

Antonio didn't understand. "Why would you care if I sold the *palacio*? We're only there a week or two a month."

"Because I was happy there. I made friends there. It felt almost like…like home."

He didn't know what she was talking about. The *palacio* was a trophy to him, nothing more. He'd bought it as a big middle finger to everyone in Spain who'd thought him worthless as a boy. But he didn't need it anymore. He was ready to move on. Strange that she'd come to think of it as home.

He licked his lips. "That still doesn't explain why you kissed me."

Hana took a deep, agonized breath. "It was

a mistake. I never should have kissed you. No matter how many years I'd wanted you."

Antonio couldn't move. She'd wanted him? For years?

"I should have quit my job right then," she said. "I've spent too long traveling from place to place, when all I've ever really wanted is a real home. A place in the world that's mine. A home no one can ever take from me."

He stared down at her.

"I never wanted a home," he said finally.

Her lips curved at the edges. "I know. You built an airline to make sure you're never stuck in one place too long. Not with one place. Not with one person."

Antonio's gaze fell to her lips. He felt a flash of heat. Everything she'd said about him was true.

So why had he been faithful to Hana—not just since their night together, but even before, since Christmas Eve?

For years, he'd tried to deny his attraction to her. He was her boss, and she was his valuable employee. But his desire for Hana had never ended. Even now, he was still racked with it, body and soul. More than ever. His nerve endings strummed with need. He felt her every movement, her every breath.

"I never should have slept with you," Hana choked out. "I should have waited for a man I could marry."

Antonio clamped down on a sudden emotion in his heart, emotion he didn't want to identify. He said harshly, "So you admit you want marriage."

"Of course I do." She looked again at the families picnicking in the April sunshine of the park, beneath the flowering cherry trees. "I want a man who will be my partner. A man who will help me build a home. Who will love our child and be there for us, every single day." Her eyes focused on Antonio. "That man won't be you."

He felt a strange twist through his solar plexus. As two men passed by on the path, Antonio saw their eyes linger on her.

Hana wouldn't be alone for long, he knew. She was too beautiful, too kind, too warm. He'd seen the way men looked at her. She could have any man she wanted, begging to bed her, to wed her, to raise her child. Starting with Ren Tanaka.

With her early pregnancy, there was a new lushness about her, not just her ripening body, but her lovely face, her dark eyes glimmering with new confidence and power. She wasn't deferential to Antonio as she'd once been. Why would she be? He was no longer her boss. No longer her lover. She'd already rejected him as her baby's father. With better reason than she even knew.

Antonio took a breath. Wasn't this what he'd wanted? So why did he feel as if he were the one being dumped?

Was it just because he'd never had a woman reject him before? Or did it go deeper than that?

"Goodbye, Antonio," Hana said quietly. This time, she didn't reach out to shake his hand. She just turned away, and he suddenly knew he might never see her again. She intended to disappear from his life, and take their baby with her. To take her sweetness and loyalty and warmth to some other, more deserving man.

The strange tension lifted from his belly to his throat, making it suddenly hard to breathe. "Wait."

Hana looked at him. "For what?"

She was close, so close. Just inches away. He could imagine her body against his. It would be so easy to take her in his arms and kiss her.

No. He couldn't. If he did, he would want

more. He cursed silently to himself. He *already* wanted more. He'd never stopped wanting more. From the moment he'd possessed her. No. From the moment he'd first hired her. Hana was his weakness, the one and only desire he hadn't been able to push aside in obedience to the coldly ruthless dictates of his brain.

But he wouldn't kiss her.

Couldn't.

It was absolutely *forbidden.*

As Antonio looked down into her brown eyes, so deep with sadness, shining beneath all the lush colors around them, he suddenly felt like all the world was bursting into spring around them. Only he was still frozen. And if she left, the cold gray winter he lived in would last forever.

His gaze fell to her full pink lips. He saw the way her even white teeth worried against the tender lower lip.

"You can't go," he said, searching her gaze. "Not until I kiss you goodbye..."

Without letting himself stop, without letting himself think, he reached for her. In the middle of the beautiful park, as cherry blossoms blew in the soft spring breeze, he cupped her face with both his hands.

He had the brief image of her wide, startled eyes in her heartbreakingly lovely face. And then he lowered his mouth to hers, kissing her with all the emotion he could not let himself think, feel or say.

He felt the tremble of her lips beneath his own, before, like a miracle, she surrendered to him with a small shivery sigh.

But almost at once, his self-control started to fray.

He wrapped his larger body around hers, holding her tight against him as he deepened the kiss, plundering her mouth until the whole world felt like it was whirling around them, as if they were the eye of the storm.

He was pulled into a vortex of desire. Suddenly he felt lost, drowning in the intensity of his need. Nothing mattered—but this—

She roughly pulled away. She looked up, her face stricken. "Don't!"

"Hana—"

"Stay away from me!"

And she turned and walked away. Antonio watched her wan figure disappear, her shoulders slumped, crossing back through the park. A cool wind blew against his face, as white petals danced in the breeze, brushing against his black cashmere coat. Burning, he was frozen, watching her.

Could he really, truly let her go?

CHAPTER FOUR

HANA FELT A lump in her throat as she walked past the bowing doorman into the Tanaka hotel. She wasn't going to let herself cry. She wasn't! Antonio wasn't worth it!

She blinked fast as her eyes burned.

She'd known all along he wouldn't want to be part of their baby's life. She'd known it even before he'd made love to her, when he'd told her outright that their affair had to be brief, forgettable and consequence-free.

So why, after telling her he couldn't be part of their baby's life, had he suddenly asked her to be his mistress—and worse, kissed her?

Her lips still burned from his kiss. Why would he do such a thing? Just to prove the power he still held over her? He'd have that power for the rest of his life, with the child that would link them until the day Hana died.

But her baby needed a real home, a real family, a real father, not someone who would leave or neglect them at his whim. Antonio would never be the man her baby needed. He'd had a vasectomy, for heaven's sake. At *eighteen*. Could he make it any more clear that he never wanted to be a father?

Better to have a clean break.

As Hana entered the hotel, she saw Ren's handsome, worried face across the lobby. She suddenly wished he could have been the father of her baby, instead of Antonio. Her best friend was a good man, smart, loyal and kind. Any child would be lucky to have him as a father.

But for Hana, he was a dear friend, nothing more. And she had to make him see that, too.

Ren took one look at her tearstained face, and his dark eyes turned grim. "What did Delacruz say? What did he do?" He set his jaw, glaring out the window. "I'm going to find him and—"

"Don't. He didn't do anything," she said wearily. "It's finished. I'll never see him again."

"You still love him." Ren's voice was flat as he looked at her. "Even after he's treated you so badly."

"No," she protested. Love? Ridiculous. Knowing what she knew, she'd have to be the stupidest woman on earth, or the worst sort of masochist, to fall in love with Antonio, and she was neither.

Something had broken him, something that left him unable to open his heart to anyone. She wasn't sure he *had* a heart.

And yet, sometimes... He did something that surprised her.

Like when her beloved grandmother had died last year from complications of dementia. Hana had been grieving her loss for years, even before her death, when Sachiko had stopped recognizing her, then stopped speaking at all. But losing the last member of her family had been a devastating blow.

And yet, initially Antonio hadn't wanted Hana to go to the funeral. He'd tried to convince her that it would be a waste of time for her to leave Madrid. "Your grandmother won't even appreciate it," he'd said firmly. "She's dead. And I need you here."

Then he'd looked at her tearstained face. And something had changed in his dark eyes.

"I'll come with you," he'd said quietly.

"It's not necessary," she'd said, her voice clogged with tears.

"I'm coming," he'd cut her off.

And he had. He'd had a million other things he should have been doing, billion-dollar deals waiting to be made, but he'd taken Hana on his private jet to rural California instead. He'd sat silently beside her at her grandmother's funeral, and afterward, when Sachiko's many friends had shyly come forward to hug Hana, whom they hadn't seen in years, Antonio had introduced himself not as her boss, but as her friend. He'd remained in California with her for two days, a comforting presence in the background, giving her the strength to go through her grandmother's things and begin arrangements to sell off the heavily mortgaged farm. Then, when it was over, he'd taken her home to Madrid.

Home. To Madrid.

A home she'd never see again now.

Hana's shoulders sagged. After everything she'd gone through today, she felt bone-tired, more tired than she'd ever been in her life.

"Are you all right?" Ren asked.

She rubbed her eyes. "Just tired."

"Don't worry, Hana," he said softly, as he looked down at her in the hotel lobby. "I'll take care of you."

The possessive look on his handsome face troubled her. She blurted out, "Ren, please, you can't think—"

He abruptly turned away. "Your satchel was

dropped off earlier. I had it taken to our best suite. You can rest there."

"Thank you." She bit her lip. "I'll pay for the room—"

"Don't be ridiculous," he said. "You're my best friend. You think I would take your money? I want to help. I am proud to have a hotel to offer you."

Hana disliked the feeling that he was offering her not just a room for the night, but himself for a lifetime. But they were best friends. She wouldn't have even questioned his offer, if she didn't fear—*know*—his feelings went deeper.

"Ren," she said gently, speaking quietly so no one else would hear, "I'm so grateful. But," she hesitated, "you have always been like a brother to me..."

He looked away. "I must go to Osaka for a few days," he said in an expressionless voice. "A business trip with suppliers. If you need me, I could cancel my trip—"

"No, I'll be fine," Hana said, relieved to put off further discussion of an issue that would be awkward at best, and at worst, horrifyingly painful for them both. It might even cost her Ren's friendship entirely, and that was a prospect she just couldn't face today. Rubbing her eyes, she confessed, "I feel like I haven't slept in a year."

He gave her a kind smile. "Come with me."

Twenty minutes later, she'd kicked off her shoes and was comfortably ensconced in a luxurious penthouse suite. He indicated her overnight bag. "If there is anything you need, anything at all, my staff will be glad to assist you."

"Thank you, Ren."

"It is the least I can do," he said, and she hated the way he looked at her. "Until I return." With a formal bow of his head, he left.

Hana exhaled, shivering with exhaustion as the aching hollows of her feet rested against the tatami mat on the floor. Picking up her bag, she silently blessed Ramon Garcia, who must have noticed she'd left her satchel and arranged to have it dropped off at the hotel. It certainly wouldn't have occurred to Antonio. No way.

But she wasn't going to think about him. She was not!

Pushing aside the sliding paper doors, she went past the main room of the suite, into the bedroom. Though exquisitely decorated in traditional Japanese style, the room still had some Western elements—like a king-size bed.

Which again, in spite of her best efforts, made her think of Antonio.

Setting down her overnight bag, she looked out the bedroom's wide windows. In the distance, she could see the bright neon lights of a busy shopping district. So different from the tranquil park where he'd just kissed her amid all the beautiful pink-and-white flowering trees.

She could still hardly believe Antonio had asked her to be his mistress—and she'd told him no.

It was the right thing to do, Hana told herself wearily, leaning her hand against the window. For Antonio, there was only one thing that was always right: strength. One thing that was always wrong: weakness.

If he crushed his opponents, it was their own fault. He'd say they had been weak, letting themselves become takeover targets or badly managing their businesses. If he bruised the hearts of his mistresses, it was the women's fault for not believing him when he told them he would never love them.

No matter how incredible their night together had been, no matter how every time she remembered their passion her body burned from her fingertips to her toes, sex wasn't enough. Antonio would never be the man she needed him to be.

Yes, she'd done the right thing, refusing to be Antonio's mistress, when it would have brought only brief pleasure at the expense of endless grief. The right thing for her. The right thing for their child.

So why did Hana feel so miserable?

Her shoulders drooped as she went into the gleaming, ultramodern bathroom and turned on the shower. She washed her hair with the orange-blossom-scented shampoo and felt the blast of water massage her skin.

Best to make the best of things. Her mother had been forty-two when Hana was born, a surprise to the married couple, who'd already spent nearly two decades teaching and traveling the world. Restless hippies both, they'd believed problems could be solved just by changing the country one lived in.

Wherever they'd traveled, Hana had been a chameleon, fitting in everywhere—and feeling like she belonged nowhere. With Hana's mixed heritage, no one looked exactly like her, certainly not her pale, red-haired father or her olive-skinned, dark-haired mother.

Her parents had had a passionate relationship—full of arguments and moaning kisses—almost like teenagers. Sometimes they'd seemed to forget they even had a daughter. Sometimes Hana had felt like *she* was the grown-up in their family.

Every time she started to make friends and actually become part of a new community, her parents would inevitably have a big fight, or declare themselves bored, and then grandly announce it was time for another "adventure" in a new country.

"It's wonderful to be free," they'd say, toasting each other with cheap wine, scorning the "poor slobs" who were "trapped in one place till death."

To Hana, without friends or roots and often feeling even excluded from her parents' tight relationship, being trapped in one place sounded like heaven. Her beloved grandmother Sachiko, a widow who was her last living grandparent, had been her only true source of stability. Whenever her parents had needed space from the onerous demands of child-rearing— "Grown-ups need time just to be romantic, darling, just for ourselves, you understand"—they'd send Hana for a few weeks to her grandmother's rural almond farm in northern California.

Sachiko was the one who'd taught her Japanese. Each time she felt her grandmother's warm arms around her, and look up into her calm, wise eyes, Hana would vow, when she grew up, she'd settle down nearby and never leave again.

But Hana had barely started college in nearby Sacramento before her father suddenly died of a stroke in Tasmania, leaving her mother in shock. No one was sure whether it was an accident when Laurel's rental car had gone off a cliff in Thailand six months later. And the very next month, her grandmother had the first onset of dementia that would eventually claim her life.

Now Hana was alone.

No, she remembered. Not alone. She'd never be alone again. She put her hand over her belly. She was going to have a baby.

Hana was going to be a mother. She'd build them a home. She had enough money so she could wait to get a job, until her baby was a few months old. She could be choosy. So she'd lost her home in Madrid. She told herself there were other places in the world.

The world is your oyster, kid, her father had always said when he was proud of her. Hana took a deep breath.

Somewhere. Somehow. She'd make the two of them a home.

As she got out of the hot shower, she dried off, brushing her long dark hair, then pulled on an ivory silk nightgown and robe from her bag. Her stomach growled, and she remembered she hadn't eaten since she'd arrived in Tokyo.

But as she was reaching to call room service, the phone rang. Nervous it might be Ren, she snatched it up. "Hello?"

"You turned off your mobile." Antonio's voice was accusing.

She gripped the receiver. "How did you find me?"

"It wasn't hard to guess you'd be staying at Tanaka's hotel," he said sardonically.

"What do you want?"

"We need to talk." His husky voice made her toes curl in spite of herself. She hardened her heart.

"We already did. In the park."

"I have more to say—"

"Don't call me again." And she hung up.

Almost immediately, the penthouse's phone began to ring again. She picked up the receiver and slammed it back without saying a word.

Then she called the front desk of the hotel and told them to hold all calls to her room.

Antonio either couldn't believe she'd turned down his *fantastic* offer to be his temporary mistress, or else he had urgent questions about business negotiations. But she didn't have to put up with his whims or worry about his ego anymore.

So she wouldn't.

Feeling too exhausted to think, Hana curled up on the enormous bed.

Her eyes flew open when she heard a hard knock on the door. *Antonio*, she thought groggily. But he couldn't know her room number. Surely none of the staff would give that information to a stranger. Stumbling to her feet, she went to the door and looked through the peephole.

She saw only a uniformed member of hotel staff.

Tightening the belt on her silk kimono robe, she opened the door the barest crack. "Yes?"

"Flowers, ma'am," the young man said, an explanation that was utterly unnecessary because five uniformed staff members stood behind him in the hallway, all holding huge full vases—red roses, pink tulips and other, more exotic flowers, enough to fill an entire shop.

"All of these—for me?" she stammered.

"Yes, miss."

"Who sent them?"

The man handed her a card. Tearing it open, Hana saw a brief sentence in Antonio's arrogant scrawl.

Talk to me.

Her heart leaped to her throat. Antonio could be ruthless and utterly single-minded when he wanted something. Had that one simple word—*No*—suddenly made him decide he wanted her? For his bed? For the boardroom? Where?

It didn't matter. He couldn't have her. He couldn't just fire her, reject her—then think he could have her back whenever and however he wanted!

"Stop," she cried, blocking them from entering her penthouse suite with the flowers. "I don't want them!"

The staff members looked at each other in bewilderment. "What shall we do with them, ma'am?" one ventured.

"I don't care—send them to the hospital—or you can have them! Do whatever you want with them, but they can't come in here!"

Closing the door in their faces, Hana exhaled, sagging against the door. But she could still smell the sweet scent of roses wafting through the air, messing with her mind. Her eyes narrowed. She started to reach for her cell phone, to call Antonio and tell him angrily what she thought of his ploy.

Then she stopped herself. That was just what he wanted. She wouldn't give him the satisfaction!

Hana paced the length of the hotel suite, trying not to think about him. She wouldn't remember all the days they'd spent together, or the night he'd taken her virginity, or the fact that she carried his child inside her. She wouldn't!

Two minutes later, the hotel suite's doorbell rang.

"Oh, for the love of..." Choking back a curse, she looked through the peephole again. Her hands trembled as she opened the door.

Another line of hotel employees stood in the hallway, weighed down with chocolates and elegant treats with the distinctive wrapping of the finest candy boutiques in Tokyo. And the uniformed staff member at the back held a silver tray spread just with different Kit Kat flavors, the *sakura* with its wrapper of delicate pink blossoms, sweet potato, wasabi, green tea and other, even more exotic flavors that she knew from experience were notoriously hard to find, exclusive only to certain cities in Japan.

She ground her teeth. This was a low blow—he was perfectly aware she had a sweet tooth. Antonio knew just how to tempt her.

No! She wouldn't give in to weakness!

"Take it all away," she told the hotel staff firmly, and shut the door again.

Hana's hands shook as she went to the low table that held a tray with a traditional tea service. She filled the kettle with water, waited, then poured hot steaming water into the delicate ceramic cup and placed herbal leaves to steep. She took deep breaths of the fragrant chamomile and tried to calm down. Peaceful, she told herself. The world is my oyster. He doesn't exist.

Then she heard another loud knock.

Setting the cup down hard on the table, she stalked to her door. Opening it, she glared at the unfortunate hotel staff, all standing there sheepishly holding large black velvet boxes.

"What now?" she snapped.

"I'm sorry, Miss Everly," the first one said unhappily, bowing, "but we were ordered to bring you this."

Glancing at the others, he gave a signal. And all five of the uniformed staff opened their flat, wide black velvet boxes at once.

Hana almost screamed.

Five necklaces sparkled at her from black velvet, each more ridiculously over-the-top than the last, necklaces that must have cost many millions of yen, that would have made Marie Antoinette blush. Brilliant diamonds, as big as robin's eggs, emeralds, sapphires, all gleamed and glistened and whispered wickedly sensual desires to her.

Against her will, she snapped back to the memory of Antonio's husky voice when her body had been naked against his in the bedroom of his *palacio.*

"I'd like to see you in jewels," he'd breathed, brushing back a long dark tendril of her hair, kissing down her collarbone. "Jewels and nothing else."

But she hadn't cared about jewels that night. Just having Antonio in her arms, after two years of helpless, hopeless desire, she'd felt like the world was exploding around her with passion and joy.

Did he really think she could be bought?

"Take them…away," she croaked out to the hotel staff.

The employees looked at each other with wide eyes. "You don't want these jewels, Miss Everly?" one ventured.

"No!" she nearly shouted. Closing the door, she sagged back against it. Why was Antonio doing this? To torture her? How dare he send her flowers, candy and jewels! Enough!

Stomping across the penthouse suite, she grabbed her cell phone from her purse. Turning it on, she dialed. She took a deep breath.

"Yes?" Antonio answered innocently on the second ring. His voice was calm, while her emotions felt like they were spiraling out of control. It enraged her further.

"Stop sending me gifts."

"Yes, I heard you sent them all back." He paused. "It surprised me that you resisted the candy."

Her cheeks burned, as she remembered all the times over the last two years when he'd teased her about her love of chocolate. All the times she'd eaten candy in the middle of the night, as he had a glass of scotch—each of them picking their own particular poison as they worked long, laborious hours on various deals. But it wasn't candy that was most forbidden. She could resist chocolate, if she needed to.

Antonio Delacruz was the most dangerous temptation. Definitely bad for her health.

Hana glared out the window toward the bright neon signs of the nearby commercial district. "How much clearer do I have to be? I don't want you in my life. Stop calling me."

"You called me," he pointed out.

"I'm hanging up."

"If you must."

"There's someone knocking at my door," she said. "If it's another ridiculous gift, I'm throwing it out the window."

"I'm hanging up now," he said smoothly.

"Good," she choked out, and flung open the door.

Hana felt her heart lift to her throat as she saw Antonio in the doorway, broad-shouldered, tall and devastatingly handsome in his suit and black coat. His cell phone was still to his ear, against his mussed black hair, and his hard jaw was scruffy as he looked right through her with his searing dark eyes.

"Will you talk to me, *querida*?" he said huskily.

CHAPTER FIVE

ANTONIO STARED DOWN at her. He couldn't remember the last time he'd pursued any woman like this. Never, not since he'd turned eighteen. But the stakes had never been so high.

Standing in her hotel room, Hana looked up at him, her brown eyes wary, one hand against the door, as if she yearned to slam it in his face. He couldn't take that chance. Bracing his hand against the door, he ruthlessly pushed into her hotel suite, closing it softly behind them.

They faced each other in the fading afternoon light of the entryway.

"What do you want?" she whispered, backing away, past the open paper doors into the main room. He followed her.

"Stop," she cried. "Kick off your shoes!"

"My shoes?"

"Japanese tradition!"

Tradition? With a snort, he started to refuse.

Then the words stopped at his lips as he saw her face.

Hana *expected* him to refuse. She thought she knew him. She didn't just think he was selfish. She thought he was broken and unredeemable. She thought he was heartless. Soulless.

He suddenly wanted to prove her wrong. To wipe away the scorn he imagined he saw in her eyes.

Antonio kicked off his handmade Italian shoes. Her eyes widened in surprise as he walked toward her on the rough reed mat. He stopped when he was just inches away from her, standing between the low-slung sofa and the wall of windows facing the city and darkening April sky.

His gaze traced her silhouette against the wide windows. She'd never looked so beautiful to him, so vulnerable—a strange thing to think, he thought wryly, when she had all the power in this moment. She had his baby inside her. The baby he'd never imagined he wanted.

But he'd discovered, to his shock, that he could not let them go—either of them. For the first time in his life, he was unable to walk away.

"You took off your shoes," Hana breathed, tilting back her head to look into his face.

Antonio gave a slight smile. "You told me to."

"I didn't expect you to do it."

"So you admit it."

"What?"

"I can surprise you." Of its own accord, his hand stretched out to trace her long dark hair, tumbling down her creamy silk robe with its elegant floral pattern. The robe's tie had become slightly loose, revealing a matching silk nightgown. His gaze traced over her bare collarbone to the neckline, which hinted at the full shape of her pregnancy-swollen breasts beneath.

Abruptly backing away, she glared at him, tightening her silk robe around her waist. "What do you want, Antonio?"

That was a strange question.

What did he want?

He thought he'd known the answer to that since he was six, when he'd returned to the orphanage after a month spent with the foster parents who'd decided not to adopt him after all. He'd cried that first night, and the older boys had bullied him for it.

Giving up all hopes of being adopted, he'd frozen his heart as a means of survival. When other children cried in the night for someone to love them, he'd become the one to tell them to shut up, to be tough, to go to sleep, so they'd be stronger to face whatever fresh hell the next day could bring.

When he'd left the orphanage on his eighteenth birthday, he'd met a pretty waitress. Isabella had been older, experienced, and was amused when Antonio fervently declared his love for her after their first night in bed. She'd been equally amused by his broken heart when she told him a few months later she was leaving him for a squat businessman three times her age.

"Sorry, Antonio." She'd shrugged. "Pierre has a new BMW and a flat in Paris. You have nothing to offer."

"Nothing but my heart," he'd choked out.

"Money is what matters. Money is what lasts." She'd patted him on the shoulder like a dog. "You're young. You'll learn."

And he had. Isabella had helped him see that, whatever awful flaw had caused him to be constantly rejected since he was born, it could be hidden by a big enough fortune.

He'd gotten a job on a small airfield and soon started his first airline with a single rickety, leased plane. He'd built his company through sheer tenacity and will. He'd succeeded where better-funded, better-connected men had failed.

And five years later, when Isabella had come

crawling back, this time he'd been the one to be amused. He'd tilted his head, coldly looking her over. "Sorry. You have nothing to offer."

Antonio didn't make excuses. He didn't give in to feelings. He controlled his own fate.

Then how to explain the inexplicable reaction now pounding through his body?

What did he want?

He wanted Hana as his mistress. But could he want more? Did he want to be a father?

A baby. Antonio tried to even imagine it. A child growing up, learning to walk and talk. Going to school. Learning sports, learning to read. A child. A son or daughter, looking up at him with smiling eyes—

"Why are you pursuing me?" Hana demanded, breaking his reverie. "I've already given you my answer. I won't be your mistress. What else can you possibly hope to gain?"

"Where is Tanaka?" he said suddenly. "Why isn't he here guarding you?"

"Ren had to leave for Osaka," she said unwillingly.

His dark eyes gleamed. "So you told him you didn't love him, and he couldn't take it."

Folding her arms over her chest, she said pointedly, "He didn't need to guard me. I didn't plan to see you again."

"We need to discuss our baby—"

"*My* baby," she said fiercely. "Just mine. It's what I want. It's what you want. So why won't you just go?"

Pacing a few long strides across the suite's luxurious main room, he stopped. He glanced out the windows, where twilight had begun to fall. He slowly turned to face her. "I can't."

He was startled to see sudden tears in her eyes. "You only want me because you think you can't have me. If I actually let you into our lives, if I tried to depend on you, you'd be gone in a second!"

"Hana—"

She turned her body away from him. "Just go. And this time, don't come back. I mean it."

Antonio's hands tightened at his sides.

How could she be so unfeeling? How could she not see how difficult this was for him? He was struggling with the question of his life: Who was he as a man? Could he be more?

Then he suddenly realized.

She didn't understand because he hadn't told her. There was only one way to change that. Just the thought made his stomach churn. But there was only one option that was worse. Leaving Hana and his unborn child behind.

Taking a deep breath, he said hoarsely, "You're right. I never wanted to be a father. That's why I had a vasectomy at eighteen."

Slowly, she turned to face him, her eyes wide.

"What did I know about fatherhood?" he continued, his jaw clenched. "I never even knew my parents. They abandoned me in a basket on the steps of a church in southern Spain the day I was born."

"What?" she breathed.

"The nuns found me. Gave me a name. Sent me to the nearest orphanage." The words came slow and halting from his lips. "When I was a few months old, I was brought home by a family who said they intended to adopt me. But they sent me back."

"Back? Why?"

He shrugged. "I never learned. Maybe I cried too much. It doesn't matter. I don't remember them." Every syllable tasted like rust in his mouth. "But I do remember the childless couple who brought me home when I was six. Then they got pregnant, and decided they didn't need me. The night they sent me back to the orphanage, I made the mistake of crying about it. The older boys said they'd give me something to cry about." Pulling back the hairline at his left temple, he revealed a raised scar. "I quit crying, all right. I was in bandages for weeks." His lips curled sardonically. "After that, no one tried to adopt me again. I made sure of that."

"Oh, no." Hana's lovely face looked stricken as she whispered, "I'm sorry."

"Don't be."

"It's not your fault—none of it is your fault!"

"I know," he lied. He shrugged. "It helped me, really. Made me stronger. Gave me ambition."

"Did you ever find out why your parents left you on those church steps?"

"No."

"There had to be some reason—"

"It doesn't matter." His voice held an edge. "I just wanted you to understand why, even at eighteen, I knew I didn't want to be a father." He thought of telling her about Isabella, but that was a step too far. He took a deep breath. "But you're pregnant. Everything has changed."

She gave a weak smile. "Because the vasectomy failed. For all you know, you might have children all over the world you've never heard about."

He rolled his eyes. "Unlikely."

"How do you know?"

"Because no woman has come to my house with a baby in her arms, begging for her fair share of my fortune."

"You really do believe the worst of everyone."

Antonio looked at her.

"Except you," he said quietly.

Coming forward, he gently traced his hands along the shoulders of her silk robe. He felt her shiver beneath his touch—or was he the one who was shivering? He dropped his hands.

"I can't abandon you, or this baby," he said in a low voice. "I might not have planned for this, but now it's happened, I can't leave my child to wonder, night after night, what flaw he could have possibly had from birth, that made him unworthy of a parent's love, unworthy of family or home."

Hana gave a choked gasp. "My baby will never feel that way! I will be there. Always."

"Yes. But he'd always wonder about his father." Emotion went through Antonio. He couldn't let this baby feel as he once had. Unworthy. Unwanted. Rejected.

"I will find someone…"

Her voice trailed off at his sharp gaze. "Tanaka?"

She shook her head. "But…but someone. A partner."

Antonio exhaled, knowing she was right. "Any man would want you," he said quietly. "But even with the best stepfather on earth, the baby will always wonder about me. Why I left. What will you tell him?"

"The truth." Her hands tightened at her sides, and her beautiful face looked down as she added, "There's no other answer."

The truth. That Antonio was a selfish, shallow playboy, more interested in his airline than his child. That he didn't have the capacity, or the desire, to commit. Not to his child. He looked at Hana. Not to her.

Unless…

Staring at her bowed head, he blinked, and the world seemed to spin on its axis. Suddenly, the solution was astonishingly clear.

The only way to get everything he wanted. To protect his child. To have Hana in his bed. Everything.

As they stood across from each other in her hotel suite, he said bluntly, "You know I don't love you."

"Of course you don't." She rolled her eyes.

"Luckily, I don't love you either. Heaven help any woman who does."

He gave a wry smile, then his expression became serious. "But you've never betrayed me. Not once. You're the one person I trust most on earth. The one I most respect."

"Thanks." Hana snorted a low laugh. "That changes nothing."

She was trying to protect herself from hurt. He knew that cynical tone. He'd used it himself. "It changes everything."

"How?"

"I want you in my bed. I want you in my company and in my life. And…" He took a deep breath. "I want to be a real father to our baby."

Her lips parted as she said hoarsely, "What are you saying?"

His lips curved as he looked down at her. "I want you to marry me, Hana."

Hana stared at him.

The twilight from the hotel penthouse's windows left a strange reddish glow on his hard, handsome face, leaving a shadow behind him on the translucent *shōji* doors of the suite.

Had he gone crazy—or had she?
Marriage?

"Is this a joke?" she choked out.

"I'm deadly serious."

She stammered, "You don't want to marry anyone."

"I just asked you." Antonio lifted his dark eyebrows. "But perhaps I didn't do it properly?"

In front of her horrified eyes, he folded his powerful body, falling to one knee before her. Taking both her hands in his own, he looked up. "Hana Everly, will you do me the honor of becoming my bride?"

"Stop it," she hissed, tugging on his hands. "Stand up."

Slowly, he rose back to his feet. His dark gaze burned through her. "Will you?"

"You're being ridiculous."

"I need an answer."

"My answer is no!"

The humor fled from his face. He said tersely, "Might I ask why?"

"For starters—you just said you don't love me!"

"Love only brings pain."

Hana thought of her parents' passionate love, their constant drama, and had to admit he maybe had a point. Then she raised her chin. "How would you even know?"

"I tried it once," Antonio said quietly. "A waitress. When I was eighteen and broke and stupid."

Hana's jaw dropped.

"You—loved someone?" she gasped. *"You?"*

"I was a virgin," he said ironically. "I thought I loved her because she took me to her bed. She told me it was hilarious and dumped me a few months later." He tilted his head. "And you, Hana? What experience have you had with love that makes you think it's necessary, or even good, for a marriage?"

She thought again about how excluded she'd felt, as her parents had focused solely on each other, on fighting and kisses, dragging their daughter around the world almost like an afterthought.

Biting her lip, she looked away.

"So," Antonio said softly. "You do have some experience with love after all."

"Not me," she said unwillingly. "But my parents. They were so in love, they—they sometimes forgot about me."

He took her hand. She felt the comfort of his touch, the heat of his palm against hers, and her whole body shivered.

She heard herself ask, "What happened to her?"

"Who?" His fingers tightened around hers.

Her cheeks burned. "The waitress."

"Ah." His lips curved. "She left me for a rich, elderly Frenchman. But she came crawling back when she heard I'd made my fortune."

"And?"

He shrugged. "I was no longer interested."

"Of course not." She looked up at his handsome, implacable face. "But marriage is a commitment for a lifetime."

"You think I don't know that?"

"Your longest love affair lasted six weeks."

His dark eyes flashed with amusement, his shoulders suddenly relaxing beneath his sleekly tailored coat. "You were paying attention?"

She bit her lip, hating that she'd revealed so much. She said defiantly, "It was my job to pay attention. To clean up your messes when you ghosted a girl and she came sobbing to me, wondering why you'd suddenly stopped calling when she'd thought she was on the fast track to earning your heart!"

"So that's why you brought Madison the camera for Christmas? You wanted her to think I was a good boyfriend?"

"For all the good it did." She scowled. "I can't believe you'd break up with someone on *Christmas morning*. Not even you."

"It seemed the only decent thing to do."

She choked a laugh. "Decent?"

"Yes. Decent." His eyes met hers. "Because when you showed up with her gift that night, I realized you were the only woman I wanted. How could I be with Madison after that?"

Hana's throat went dry.

"I've been faithful to you ever since then." He shook his head ruefully. "Against my will. I had no choice. Because I wanted no other woman. Just you."

Her heart was pounding. "Why didn't you say anything?"

"I couldn't let myself seduce you."

"Why?"

"You were too important. I was afraid if I took you to my bed, I'd end up breaking your heart, and then my company would lose the best damn secretary in the world."

"Then you fired me anyway."

Antonio gave a rueful laugh. "Not my finest moment. Can I hire you back?"

"I haven't decided," she said faintly. What was happening? The hotel suite was spinning around her. Antonio, proposing marriage? Was this all a dream?

"Marry me, Hana," he said in a low voice. "I'll be faithful to you until the day I die."

"How can you be sure?"

"You're the only woman I desire." He cupped her cheek. "The one I trust."

She shivered at his nearness, trying not to notice the weight and warmth of his hand against her skin, sending a spiral of sparks down her body. She was suddenly aware that she wore only a creamy silk negligee and robe against her skin. She wasn't even wearing panties beneath.

His hand moved slowly down the edge of her bare neck. He repeated, "Marry me."

She trembled as he pulled her into his arms. Standing in the middle of the penthouse suite, her feet bare on the tatami mat, Hana tilted her head to look up at his handsome face.

"You're going to have my baby." He gently placed his large hand against her belly, sliding over the sensual silk of her robe. "You belong to me," he said huskily. Lowering his head toward hers, he whispered, "As I belong to you…"

Her knees went weak as his lips possessed hers. He was so much larger than she was, so broad-shouldered and strong. She surrendered to his embrace, lost in sensation as their kiss intensified.

His hands cupped the back of her head, lightly brushing down her long dark hair as he caressed slowly down her back, causing the silk to slide over her naked skin.

Pressed against his fully clothed body, she felt his heat and strength, which he tempered and held back, holding her as if she were a precious treasure. Her nipples tightened as they brushed against his suit and tie, her swollen breasts sensitive and heavy. Tension coiled low and deep inside her.

How long had her body cried out to be in Antonio's arms, held with such passionate tenderness? How long had her soul thirsted to hear words like this from anyone?

No wonder the penthouse seemed to spin around her. She was dreaming. She had to be dreaming!

And she wasn't sure she ever wanted to wake up…

Her hands wrapped around his shoulders as she kissed him back with all the longing in her heart. As he deepened the embrace, she felt a sudden urgency, a need to have him closer, to block out the small voice in the back of her mind that was shouting that she needed to stop this, stop it before it was too late. Reaching under his dark cashmere coat, she lifted it off his shoulders and pulled it down his back.

She felt his approval, his answering need. Before the coat had even dropped to the floor, he was yanking off his tie and jacket, unbuttoning his cuffs. Never breaking the kiss, she reached to undo his shirt, desperate to feel the bare skin of his hard-muscled chest beneath her fingertips. The last button caught. Urgently, she yanked hard on the shirt, feeling it finally rip and give way as that too dropped to the floor.

With a low growl, he lifted her up in his arms, against his bare chest, and carried her into the bedroom. Looking up at him breathlessly, she ran her hand along his powerful muscles, lightly dusted with dark hair. His tanned skin felt like satin beneath her hands as she traced over the hard curves of his pecs, brushing his taut nipples with her fingertips, and down farther, to the flat, hard plane of his belly.

Releasing her, he let her slide down his body, the silk caressing her skin, and set her to her feet.

They faced each other in front of the enormous bed.

Reaching out, he undid the belt of her robe, pulling it off her shoulders. As it fell softly to the floor, he wrapped his arms around her, kissing her neck. With a soft gasp, Hana closed her eyes, letting her long dark hair tumble down her back, brushing against the bare skin of her shoulders. Her nipples felt exquisitely sensitive against her nightgown, which left her arms and collarbone bare.

"You belong to me, Hana," he whispered against her skin. "Say it."

"I…" She caught her breath, her heart pounding. It was true. She belonged to him. She had from the day they'd met, when he'd given her that carelessly charming smile and said, *So I hear you're the best secretary in the world and I'm a fool if I don't hire you immediately.* But if she told him she belonged to him, if she said the words aloud, she was afraid she would be lost—lost forever. What next?

Would she agree to marry him?

Raise their child together?

Fall in love with him?

No. That would be a disaster. As crazy as her own parents' marriage had been, at least they'd both loved each other. Hana couldn't imagine the lonely desperation of being trapped in a marriage with a man she loved, who didn't love her back.

And how long would she be able to keep her heart cold, if she married Antonio, and every day, she watched him be a loving father to their child, and every night, he made love to Hana with fiery passion in their bed? How long?

"Say it," he commanded.

Wordlessly, she shook her head.

Antonio gave a sensual smile. Lowering his head to hers, he whispered, "You will…"

His kiss was gentle, deepening until it was so passionate, it was almost overwhelming. She gasped as explosive pleasure ricocheted from her scalp to the hollows of her feet.

Reaching up, she held him tightly. But she couldn't give in to the temptation of being his wife. Perhaps once he possessed her again, he'd lose interest. Soon, perhaps tomorrow, he would remember that he was a workaholic playboy who had no interest in marriage or children. He'd leave her and the baby in peace.

But until then…

She couldn't stop. She couldn't let go. No one else had ever made her feel like this, so alive.

"Querida," he whispered against her lips. And she realized he was trembling. Was it possible

that he felt the same overwhelming desire beyond reason that she did? No, surely not with all his experience. And yet...

"Kiss me," she breathed. She didn't want to talk. She didn't want to think.

He held her tight, plundering her mouth with his own, the tip of his tongue teasing and luring her until she no longer knew where he ended and she began. She felt him pull the straps of her nightgown from her shoulders, and it slipped down her body in a soft blur of silk, leaving her naked in front of him in the darkened bedroom.

He slowly looked her over, from her pregnancy-swollen breasts to the soft curve of her belly and hips. His hot gaze lifted, as he unbuttoned his black trousers and pulled off the rest of his clothes, until he stood proudly naked in front of her, his shaft huge and hard.

Falling back on the enormous bed, he pulled her against him, kissing her. Rolling her beneath him, he kissed slowly down her body, cupping her breasts, suckling her until she gasped with pleasure, her back curving up from the bed. She felt the roughness of his tongue swirling against the tight, aching flesh of her nipple, and panted for breath, nearly exploding.

"No, my sweet," he murmured. "Not yet."

He moved down her body, gentle over her belly, before he gripped her hips. He lowered his head and she squeezed her eyes shut, feeling dizzy.

He teased her, kissing along the edge of her hip as his hands spread her thighs wide. She felt the warmth of his breath, causing prickles of need to rush up and down her body. Lowering his head, he took a long deep taste.

She gasped, shaking. The pleasure was almost too great, and she tried to twist her hips away. But he was relentless. The tip of his tongue moved delicately against her, twisting and swirling around her. He held her down, tempting her to accept the pleasure, working her with his tongue as he pressed a thick finger inside her, then another, pushing deeper, wider, until she exploded.

As she cried out, he moved, lifting his body to position his hips between her legs. Even as she was still shaking with explosions of pleasure, he took a deep breath, then pushed himself inside her, thrusting his full length so deep, deep, deep inside her, until the blazing fire consumed her, and she cried out his name.

Antonio held his breath. He was so deep inside her. He wanted to make this last. He was good at this; he always had been. He'd always had stamina. He could make sex last as long as he wanted. All he had to do was remove his mind from his body. All he had to do was not care.

He would make Hana agree to marry him. He would possess her forever. He just had to stay in control. He had to make her lose her mind. Make her surrender.

But as he felt Hana tighten around him, something felt different. *He* felt different. Shocked, he tried to pull his mind away, his heart, and not care.

But for the first time in his life, it didn't work.

He felt everything, every exquisite sensation. The brush of her soft body beneath his. The satin of her skin. The vision of her long dark hair spread across the pillow, the way her full plump breasts swayed against his arms straining to hold himself up from her.

And most of all, the pure ecstasy of being inside her, rammed into her hot tight sheath. No— he couldn't—he scrambled to hold himself back. *I feel nothing, I feel nothing—*

Then he heard her scream his name as she exploded a second time, felt the rake of her fingernails against his back as she tightened around the full length of his shaft. Against his will, his body rushed forward like a careening train, leaving him helpless against the pleasure as with a shocked cry, he exploded, pouring himself inside her.

One thrust. That was all his famous stamina had been good for with Hana. *One.*

Still panting for breath, overwhelmed and stunned, he collapsed beside her on the bed, pulling her into his arms.

As reason slowly returned, he tried to understand what had just happened. He'd never had sex without a condom before. He'd never known how intense it would be. That had to be why he'd exploded like some teenaged virgin. Wasn't it?

Antonio looked down at Hana, nestled naked and warm against his chest. Her eyes were closed, her lovely face rosy, her expression hallowed by joy. She sighed with happiness, pressing against him. Kissing her sweaty temple tenderly, he wrapped his arms around her.

He knew he'd satisfied her. But he'd wanted to do so much more. He'd wanted to impress her, to dazzle her, to bring her to fulfillment not just twice, but three or four times.

Instead, he'd been the one who'd been dazzled and overwhelmed, by a girl barely more than a virgin. He took a deep breath. He didn't understand what had happened.

But he could never let it happen again.

Antonio had to remain in control. Always. Not just of others. Of himself most of all.

Strength came from not caring about other people. If you felt nothing, you could withstand injury. If you were impervious to pain, if you didn't give a damn about anyone, you could make it through anything. No one could hurt you.

He looked down at her, cuddled against his shoulder, naked and soft and warm.

One thrust.

She'd made him explode with one thrust.

The changing neon lights from the city below left patterns across her soft skin. He cupped a hand over her naked breast, and was awed when he felt himself start to stir again, when it had been only minutes since he'd had her.

Eyes still closed, she gave a soft, satisfied sigh, cuddling against him. He wondered if he'd ever get enough of her—if he'd ever be truly satisfied, or he'd always feel like a starving man when she was near.

How could he already want her again?

An incredulous smile lifted to his lips. Losing control over his body had been—interesting, at least. How had she made sex so thrilling and new? In the past, it had felt like satisfying an appetite, nothing more. But Hana made his body react in ways he'd never experienced. Even now, when he should have been completely satiated, lying naked beside her, he was once again hard as a rock.

Why? How? Because he'd wanted her for so long? The delayed gratification of finally possessing her after months of repressed desire—and the years before that?

He didn't know the reason, but she made everything feel new.

And he was going to marry her. No other man would be able to touch her—ever. She was his alone.

She would agree to marry him. Soon. Tomorrow, if he could convince her. And he would. When had he ever had trouble sweeping a woman off her feet?

When had he ever had to try?

Now. And he would. He would seduce her with everything he had.

Antonio started to turn away, to reach for his phone, intending to make plans—

Hana's eyes fluttered open as she yawned.

"Don't go," she whispered, reaching for him. "Stay with me all night."

No man alive could have resisted her sweetly pleading voice, her softly enticing body, her breasts and hips half-covered by a cotton sheet. He pulled her back against his chest.

"I'm never leaving you again," he said huskily, and he meant every word.

CHAPTER SIX

HANA WOKE WITH a start to discover the gentle pink light of morning suffusing the hotel suite's bedroom. A smile was on her lips, then she remembered with a gasp everything that had happened last night, and looked next to her on the bed.

It was empty.

Antonio was gone.

A crushing disappointment filled her, even as she told herself it was exactly what she'd known would happen. Just as soon as he'd gotten what he wanted, he'd left.

If anything, she should be surprised he'd stayed so long. He'd made love to her three times last night. Her cheeks burned, remembering. Four times, if you counted the interlude in the shower. Her whole body ached with the sweet exhaustion of pleasure. She'd never imagined anyone could make her feel that good, over and over and over. No wonder all those women went so crazy over him. And no wonder he would not commit to any of them for long. He was probably already on the other side of Tokyo, focusing back on the negotiations for the codeshare with Iyokan Airways. His company was his only true love, his family and religion, and now that he'd possessed Hana so thoroughly, Antonio had moved on with—

"Buenos días, querida."

Her lips parted in a gasp as she saw him entering the bedroom with a tray. He was wearing only a white terry cloth robe, which set off his tanned skin and gorgeous body to perfection. As he came closer to the bed, she saw he'd showered and freshly shaved.

"G-good morning," she stammered, unsure how to react. Even though he'd promised her he'd stay the entire night, she'd never imagined he'd actually do it. He never stayed the night with any of his mistresses. He either came home, or kicked them out, with the excuse of an early morning meeting that was, to be fair, always true.

"I thought you'd be hungry." Antonio set down the silver tray beside her on the bed. She saw a full breakfast of eggs and fruit and toast and other delicious things, beside a pretty red rose in a bud vase. Then she took a deep breath, and frowned.

"Um…thank you?"

"You're welcome." He gave her a sensual smile. "Coffee?"

Her stomach, which had been strangely finicky for the last few weeks for a cause she now knew was morning sickness, immediately rebelled, and she shook her head. "Actually," she said, careful not to sniff again, "Could you take that coffee into the other room? It…"

He looked at her. "The smell makes you sick?" He immediately grabbed the carafe and left the suite. He returned empty-handed a moment later. "Orange juice?"

"Thank you."

He poured it, then handed her the glass. Now that the coffee smell was gone, she took a deep breath, inhaling his delectable scent of clean male and woodland spice and something indefinably him. Now *that* smelled good to her. Too good, even.

He sat down on the edge of the bed, looking down at her tenderly. "How did you sleep?"

"Not long enough," she said, blushing a little.

Antonio gave her a wicked grin. "Perhaps we'll need to take a nap later, eh?"

Based on the way he was looking at her, she doubted it would involve much actual sleep.

How could she already want him again? How was it possible? Was she really such a wanton?

Yes, she realized, looking up with a shiver into his dark Spanish eyes. She was utterly a wanton where Antonio Delacruz was concerned.

Oh, this wasn't good at all. She'd believed with all her heart that one more night would make him lose interest, and stop him from trying to tempt her with dreams that couldn't possibly come true—dreams of marrying him, of raising their child together. She couldn't let herself hope, when after two years of watching him, she knew it was a hopeless fantasy. Men like Antonio never changed!

But as she felt his hot gaze on her, she felt the answering tremble of desire across her body. She quickly set down her orange juice. "Aren't you heading back into the office this morning? To finish the Iyokan deal?"

He shook his head. "I thought I might show you around Tokyo."

Wide-eyed, Hana looked at him, then her lips lifted at the edges. "I've been here a few times. I speak Japanese fairly well. And you're going to show *me* around?"

He looked disgruntled. He was accustomed to being the one with all the answers, the one in control.

But after last night… Hana thought of the first time they'd made love, when he'd exploded almost the very moment he'd pushed inside her, when she was still lost in the swirl of her own pleasure. He was a famous lover. That couldn't have been his plan.

Something had made him lose control.

Though perhaps this was a normal changeup in his repertoire. How would she know? She'd been screaming his name—she blushed at the memory—so he'd known there was no reason to wait. The etiquette of sex was still a mystery to her. But he'd certainly made it last longer the next three times. *Lots* longer. They'd been in bed the first time. After that, it had been against the wall. In the shower. Against the windows overlooking the neon lights. Her eyes became unfocused as a flash of heat went through her, lost in the memories.

"We can't stay here," Antonio said huskily. She blinked, her cheeks warming as she paused chewing her toast. Was she that transparent? Could he see that she'd been picturing just that?

"Of course not," she said hurriedly. "You think I want to stay in bed all day?"

He looked at her knowingly, and her blush deepened.

Then, shaking his head, he scowled. "The waiter wouldn't let me pay for room service. Apparently your dear friend Tanaka," his voice held an edge, "gave his staff orders that this penthouse suite is not to be charged for anything."

She couldn't imagine a proud man like Antonio allowing another man to pay his way. Particularly not someone he saw as a rival. Biting her lip, she said awkwardly, "Ren is a dear friend…"

"We will move to my hotel room tonight," he cut her off.

"It's not up to you." She lifted her chin. "I can sleep where I please."

Antonio gave her an easy smile. "Of course." He moved closer to the bed in his white terry cloth robe, and she had a flash of tanned, powerful legs and his hard-muscled chest. "Do you want more breakfast?"

Looking down at the tray, Hana realized she'd somehow gobbled it all down. "No…"

His sensual lips curved. "Perhaps I'm being hasty to want to tour the sights of Tokyo. We could stay in, and order more…"

Pushing the tray aside, she jumped out of bed, snatching up her silk robe, which had been left in a puddle on the floor last night when they'd… but she wasn't going to think about that. She wrapped the robe around herself and tied it firmly. "How did the negotiations end yesterday?"

"A total disaster," he said cheerfully.

"Don't you want to try to save the deal? We've been working on it for months!"

Antonio shook his head.

"You're just letting it go?" she asked in astonishment.

He looked down at her, as they stood together next to the enormous bed with its tangled sheets warmed by golden light. He murmured, "I have a different priority today."

She didn't have to ask what it was. He'd made his determination plain. But it seemed incredible to her that Antonio Delacruz was putting his desire to marry her as a greater priority than the business deal that would give him routes into Asia. She snorted. "Are you trying to impress me by giving up the deal just to spend time with me?"

"Would that work?"

"No," she lied, "and I think it's ridiculous

when you know how important this deal is to CrossWorld Airways. Do you want to expand into Asia or not?"

Antonio came so close to her, their bodies almost touched. He looked down at her, his darkly handsome face serious. "I want to marry you."

Her mouth went dry, and with an effort, she turned away. "This isn't a game!"

"You're the only one who seems to think it is."

"I'm not going to marry you, Antonio. Never ever!"

For a moment, his dark eyes looked vulnerable. Then a veil came down over his gaze. "We'll see."

She must have imagined that look in his eyes, she decided. Antonio Delacruz had no feelings. He was heartless. He prided himself on it.

But he was starting to get to her. Could Antonio really care about this baby? Could he actually commit to raising a child? Hana shivered. Could he commit to *her*?

She was still stunned by what he'd told her of his childhood. He'd always been notoriously closed-lipped about his past. What people knew about him was mostly the business legend, how he'd taken one small leased airplane in the south of Spain and turned it into an empire through hard work and grit. He'd taken big chances, and somehow made those risks pay off.

But no one knew the story of the newborn baby left on the church steps. The young boy who'd been taken home by two different families, then heartlessly rejected. The teenager who'd offered his heart to his first lover, only to be spurned.

No wonder he'd never wanted children. No wonder his company was his only family and money his way of keeping score. Who could blame him for having no heart after that?

"Why is marriage suddenly so important to you?" she asked. "You've never wanted it before."

"I told you. My child must always know they were wanted. He—or she—will have a name. A home."

A home. Emotion hit her. How could she refuse? Hana took a deep breath.

"Fine," she said quietly. "You can be in our baby's life. You're the father. The baby can have your name."

Antonio's shoulders seemed to relax slightly. He looked at her. "And you will marry me."

But on that precipice, she shivered with fear. Allowing him to help raise their baby was one thing. But to willingly promise to spend the rest of her life with a playboy who'd never love her? Her heart wasn't as cold as his.

But he was offering her everything she'd once dreamed about. A real home for their baby. Marriage. A settled family. Stability. Security.

"Where would we live?" she heard herself ask in a small voice.

"Madrid," he said huskily. "In the house you already love."

Madrid. She looked away, her heart in her throat. She thought of the *palacio*, all the people she'd come to care about, the company's world headquarters, the warm Spanish sun and palm trees rustling softly in the wind. Madrid. "I… I don't know."

Silence fell.

"Get dressed," he said suddenly.

Surprised, she looked at him. "For what?"

Antonio gave her a crooked smile. "Didn't you offer to show me the sights of Tokyo?"

"Yes, but…what about the Iyokan deal?"

"It can wait." He went back to the foyer, returning with an expensive designer overnight bag. He flashed her a grin. "Garcia delivered this an hour ago when I called for room service."

She watched as he opened the bag. "What are you doing?"

Glancing through the window at the bright sun and blue sky, he pulled out a black jacket, white button-down shirt and black trousers. "You're going to show me what you love about this city." His lips curved as he looked up at her, then glanced suggestively at the bed. "Unless you'd rather linger…"

"No," she said quickly. Any more time in bed would surely end with his engagement ring on her finger. She had to resist. *Had* to. Until he came to his senses and realized marriage was the last thing he wanted. In the meantime she couldn't let her heart talk her into surrendering her body, her soul and her life!

Safer to be out on the streets, where she wouldn't be tempted into wicked pleasures that might lure her into becoming his bride.

Or so Hana thought.

But for the next few hours, as she took Antonio to see the most famous tourist sights of Tokyo, even convincing him to leave his driver and bodyguard behind so they could experience the sidewalks and the notoriously crowded subways, she wasn't so sure.

Because she'd never seen Antonio like this, so

attentive, so good-natured, so darkly charming as he told her amusing stories about how he'd broken into the aviation business, long before they'd met, and the foibles of wealthy acquaintances, stories she'd never heard as his secretary. She was dazzled by his graveled, sexy voice, with its slight Spanish accent, and the burn of his dark eyes every time he looked at her. She kept thinking that any moment, he'd remember the critical importance of the business deal, and announce his departure. But he didn't.

They visited shrines, parks, museums, peered at buildings constructed for the Olympics, then the noodle museum and lunch. He was always beside her, his hand protectively at the ready. Later, as they took a boat meandering down a waterway that had once been a moat around Edo Castle, she started to shiver in her pale pink sundress and sandals, and he'd pulled off his jacket and wrapped it around her shoulders. But she wasn't shivering from the cold.

Looking up at him as their small boat went slowly down Chidorigafuchi Moat beneath the blooming cherry trees, Hana's heart was filled with yearning. How she wished this could be real—that he could be her husband, and she could be his wife, that they could be partners, forever and ever. But she knew the risks. What if he changed his mind? Or worse—what if she gave him her heart and he rejected it?

"What are you thinking?" Antonio said softly. Another thing he'd never said to her before, and that she doubted he'd ever said to any woman.

"Nothing," she said, looking away. She heard his phone ring from his jacket pocket. Again. It had been ringing incessantly since they'd left the restaurant. "Oh." Reaching into his jacket still hanging over her shoulders, she handed him the phone, careful not to look at it so she didn't seem like she was invading his privacy. "Here."

Taking it, Antonio frowned.

Hana shrank a little, watching him. Who was calling him? Few people had his direct number. Was it another woman? He'd had many mistresses in the past. And time after time, she'd seen him treat those women so casually, discarding them like drive-through wrappers after lunch. Easily consumed, easily forgotten, easily replaced.

Glancing at the phone, Antonio turned it off without comment. He gave it back to her. "Sorry."

"It's fine." Putting it back in the jacket pocket, she told herself she wasn't going to ask. She had no intention of marrying him, so why would she care who called him?

She was grateful, in fact. It reminded her why she had to stay strong and resist his marriage proposal.

Because she was tempted. After they reached the end of the boat ride, as he held out his hand to help Hana out, she couldn't help but imagine what it would be like if every day could be like this. Having a home together. Working together. Raising a child together. Being happy.

But this feeling couldn't last. Even if Antonio could be faithful to her as he vowed, he was a workaholic who loved only his company. He'd never make room in his life to be a full-time husband and father. That wouldn't change. Ever.

Although, she suddenly realized, he'd just given up a critical business deal, just to spend the day with her and see the sights of Tokyo…

"What about shopping?" Antonio asked, his dark eyes crinkling in a smile. "I heard Tokyo has some of the best luxury shops in the world."

She paused. "Yes, it does. Why? Do you need something?"

"Yes," he said firmly. "I do."

Hours later, they came out of yet another lavish Ginza boutique, a toy store so enormous it was five stories high. Going out onto the main shopping avenue of Chuo-Dori, Hana was still shaking her head.

"The baby won't be born until October," she chided. "And this is too much! Don't you think you should wait?"

"Wait for what?"

"You haven't even seen a scan yet. I'm only ten weeks pregnant."

He stopped. "Did the doctor you saw hint there might be a problem?"

"No, she said everything looked perfect. But it just seems—"

"What?"

"Like tempting fate!"

Looking down at her, he said gruffly, "I make my own fate."

That was certainly true. Hana shook her head with a laugh. "Toys, baby clothes. The most expensive baby stroller I've ever seen. I've seen cars that cost less! It's just a good thing the shops deliver, or you'd have needed to hire a van and staff to carry it all."

"I wanted to buy more." Standing beside her on the busy sidewalk, he looked down at her seriously. "I wanted to buy things for you. Why won't you let me?"

Hana looked away, feeling her cheeks burn. "I'm not your responsibility."

"I'd like you to be." The intensity of his dark gaze burned through her. She couldn't bear it. Tugging on his hand, she started walking. They passed other lavish luxury department stores and boutiques. Glancing down the street at the enormous, exclusive Bulgari flagship on the corner, he stopped her. "I want to buy you a ring, any ring you like, the biggest damn diamond in the entire store."

"I don't need a big diamond," she objected. All around them, Tokyo's traffic whirled past, making her dizzy.

"I'd give anything," Antonio said gruffly, "to get down on one knee and propose marriage in any way that would make you say yes. With a twenty-carat diamond ring, a sapphire, an emerald—even a damn ring from a gumball machine." He looked at her. "What would it take, Hana? Tell me. Whatever it is, I can do it. Just tell me."

Her heart was in her throat. Her eyelashes fluttered, brushing her cheek as she looked down at her own hands. She couldn't look him in the eye. He couldn't know how close she was to falling. If he had any idea of how tempted she was to surrender—

"Mr. Delacruz!" a voice called loudly. *"Señor!"*

Turning, she saw Ramon Garcia's hulking form waving at them through the crowded sidewalks. "There you are," the man panted. "We've been looking for you. All over. The lawyers are frantic."

"What do you want?" Antonio demanded, clearly annoyed.

"It's—the Iyokan deal." The muscular bodyguard leaned over, gasping to catch his breath. She wondered how long he'd been running. "Another company made—an offer. Iyokan says if they don't get a—sweetened deal—by the end of the day, they're going to walk. Please." He waved desperately toward the street. "The car is around the corner. Come now."

"I turned off my phone for a reason," Antonio said coldly. "Tell the lawyers I'm busy." And he turned back to Hana. "What's next?"

She stared at him, thinking of the hundreds of hours she'd spent over the last few months, helping him assess and prepare the legal and financial documentation for the negotiations. This deal was CrossWorld Airways's entrée into the

Asian market, the key to make his company a truly global power.

"Are you crazy?" she demanded. "Go! Go now!"

"I don't care. Let it fail." Antonio looked at her steadily. "I'm not going anywhere. I'm here. For you."

Her jaw dropped.

He was truly willing to fail, and let a competitor win in his place? Just to impress her? Just to *woo* her?

No. No way.

"Forget that." Hana's eyes narrowed. "We're going. Right now."

"We?" Antonio blinked. "But I thought—"

"You thought I'd let the deal we've both killed ourselves over for months just disappear up in smoke? No way!" She turned to the bodyguard. "We're coming now."

She heard Antonio's ragged intake of breath.

"Querida..." he breathed, and, pulling her into his arms, he looked down at her with such pure joy that it melted her right through. She beamed back at him, and then her smile slid from her face.

Oh, she was in so much trouble.

CHAPTER SEVEN

TWO HOURS LATER, as Antonio walked out of the boardroom with the Iyokan Airways deal signed and delivered, he looked down at the amazing, intoxicating woman beside him.

"We did it," he said, still slightly dazed.

Hana turned to him, smiling. "*You* did it."

Antonio shook his head. She was the one who'd known every detail necessary to hammer out the negotiations and get everything signed. Her beauty hadn't hurt either, or her fluency in Japanese. The CEO of Iyokan Airways had obviously been charmed. Even now, as they walked out of the office toward the elevator, trailing lawyers in their wake, Antonio still wondered if the other airline had made the deal in order to partner with CrossWorld Airways—or to partner with Hana Everly.

Either way, with one stroke, Antonio's airline now had the international reach he'd always dreamed of.

"The deal was signed because of you," Antonio said quietly.

"I couldn't let you lose it. Not when it means so much to you."

He thought of how hard she'd worked, at his side, night and day. "And you."

"I love our company, too," she said simply.

Our company.

He'd never thought of it that way before.

"We're all going to celebrate," Emika Ito, the pretty young director of the Japanese lead team, called out to them. "Come join us!"

"Thanks, but we have plans," Antonio replied automatically, not looking away from Hana's beautiful face.

"We'll be at the hotel bar in Ginza if you change your mind!"

"What plans?" Hana asked him.

Plans? Antonio's only plan was that he wanted to feel like this forever, triumphant after their business deal, with this sensual, brilliant woman in his arms. No one else could have done it— none but Hana.

"You're right. The company isn't just mine," he heard himself say suddenly. "It's ours."

"I know," she said cheerfully. "You couldn't possibly succeed without me." Then she saw his expression. Her forehead furrowed. "What are you trying to tell me?"

Yes, what? His heart was suddenly pounding. He could hardly believe he was saying it. But he slowly said, "You know this company is my life. My family. But you and the baby are part of that now. You should be with me."

"You—" Licking her lips, she said, "You want to hire me back as your secretary?"

"Not my secretary." He took a deep breath, then plunged in. "My full partner."

Her lips parted. "Wh-what?"

Antonio took her hands in his own. "Maybe I can't offer you love like in the fairy tales. But we could have an incredible marriage. We'll work together, create a worldwide empire—a legacy that someday our child will inherit."

Her warm brown eyes met his. They looked equal parts terrified and dazzled. "We'll spend our days together, as a team? Working together like before?"

"Better than before. This time, we'll be partners. Our family. Our company." Running his hands through her long dark hair, he whispered, "I can imagine nothing better than spending our days together running our empire, and our nights setting the world on fire."

He heard her gasp. Her cheeks were pale as she looked up at him in shock. "You'd give me half your company—just like that?"

Antonio could hardly believe it himself. His heart was pounding. He felt almost sick if he let himself think about it that way. His company meant everything to him. Even now, part of his heart was screaming that he couldn't risk this, couldn't, not even with someone he trusted as much as Hana. His company was everything he had.

But what risk? He needed her in his company. He needed her at his side, slaying dragons. Almost as much as he needed her in his bed.

He wanted to marry her. If she refused this, he did not know what more he could offer her.

Standing by the elevator on the top floor of the Tokyo office, he looked at her. "What do you say, Hana?" he asked in a low voice. "Will you have me?"

"If you would offer me half of your company, then some part of you must—"

She stopped.

He prompted, "Must?"

"Must...really want to marry me."

He had the strange feeling that she'd been

about to say something else. "How much clearer can I be?"

Hana looked up at him, her eyes shining. "I thought I knew you," she whispered. "But maybe I don't. Because the man I knew could never do what you've just done."

Antonio felt a drop of cold sweat go down his back. Half his company. How could he have offered her that? How?

But he had to win. He could not lose Hana. She was the heart of CrossWorld Airways. She was the mother of his unborn child.

"Does that mean yes?" he asked quietly.

Her eyes were suddenly full of tears. "What if you regret it?"

"I won't," he said harshly, praying he wouldn't.

The elevator dinged as the door slid open. Behind them, more lawyers were coming out of the boardroom with their assistants and briefcases. Grabbing Hana's hand, Antonio pulled her inside the elevator, away from prying eyes.

Taking her into his arms, he whispered, "Say you'll be mine."

He could feel her trembling, tottering on the brink of surrender.

"Just...just let me think," she breathed.

Antonio's mind whirled. They were both exhilarated after signing the deal. Perhaps tomorrow she'd have a clearer head. Perhaps tomorrow, Ren Tanaka would be back from Osaka and convince her she could do better than Antonio. He looked down at her.

Which she could.

Cupping her face in both his hands, he vowed, "I'll make you happy, Hana. We'll have a marriage. A home. I'll be a good husband and father. Everything you ever wanted. I swear it. Marry me. Marry me now. Today."

For a moment, he thought she was still going to say no, and his heart thundered in his chest. He'd never let himself be so vulnerable, not since he was eighteen. In fact, he'd created his whole life to make sure he never felt vulnerable like this.

Hana took a deep breath.

"Yes," she said quietly.

"You will?" Antonio felt a rush he'd never felt before. Every business deal he'd ever made, even the first one that had allowed him to lease a plane for little more than a promise of a percentage of future profits, paled compared to this. He needed Hana in his bed. Tonight. Knowing he would possess her, now and for always.

He needed her as his wife.

* * *

And so it was that an hour later, they were signing the document in a plain civil registration in a government office in the city. Hana seemed slightly bewildered, as if she wasn't sure how it had happened so fast. But with Tokyo's straightforward marriage laws, there was no need to wait. Neither of them had ever been married before. They'd just needed passports, his driver and Ramon Garcia as witnesses, and a simple document from their embassies. They wore the same clothes as when they'd left Tanaka's hotel that morning, Antonio in a white shirt and black trousers, Hana in her pale pink sundress, clutching the tiny bouquet of cherry blossoms he'd impulsively bought from the flower shop across the street.

And just like that, it was done. They were married.

After a lifetime of being absolutely sure he would never, *could* never, marry anyone, he could hardly believe how easy it had been to marry Hana.

They left the small government office and came out into the fading afternoon light, Antonio holding the marriage document with one hand and Hana's arm with the other. As they came out of the building, a beam of light fell on her, and he stopped.

Golden light caressed her long dark hair like a halo, frosting her soft cheeks, her pale pink sundress and sandals. She looked fresh-faced, sweet and innocent as a country girl—except for the big diamond ring on her finger, which he'd insisted on buying at Cartier en route to their civil ceremony. It wasn't the biggest diamond in the store, but it had been the most expensive, because it was perfect.

Like Hana, Antonio thought, dazzled. Perfect in every way.

And now she was his—forever. He shivered. He couldn't wait to get her into bed. He'd made love to her four times last night, but he still wanted her to the point of madness. It was insane, the grip she had over him. Normally that sense of lost control might have scared him. But that was nothing.

Not compared to the fact that he'd just married her without a prenuptial agreement.

He could hardly have asked for one, after his big speech about wanting to share his company with her. And the last thing he'd wanted was to wait for his lawyers, when he'd been desperate to marry her today before the municipal office closed. They'd barely squeaked in before closing time as it was. He hadn't wanted to give her a night to think it over or change her mind—especially since he'd heard her call Ren Tanaka as they left the skyscraper in Marunouchi, leaving him a message about her hasty wedding.

But now, thinking of what he'd just done, Antonio felt ice slide down his spine.

He'd promised her half his company. He'd married her without a prenup.

Without his airline, Antonio was nothing. He was still that dirty, worthless little orphan no one wanted, no use to anyone, not even his own family—

With a deep breath, Antonio pushed the old fear aside. He could trust Hana, damn it. She would never leave him. She'd never try to wrest control of CrossWorld Airways from him. She would respect his decisions. At least she always had before.

Before he'd given her everything…

"Congratulations, you two!" Ramon Garcia exclaimed, interrupting Antonio's unsettling reverie. "How are you going to celebrate? Join the team at the bar? Wait until they hear!"

Antonio's gaze traced from the delicate corner

of Hana's neck to the full curves of her breasts. "I have something else in mind."

All he wanted to do was get back to his own lavish hotel suite—far from Tanaka's hotel— and make love to his wife.

His wife!

"Oh, please." Hana turned to him with her big brown eyes. "Can't we meet with the others?" She added wistfully, "I'd love to celebrate with everyone…"

There was no way he could deny her anything right now.

"If you wish it, *querida*," he agreed, and Garcia and Haruto Nakamura, the Japanese driver, cheered. His wife, with an adorable smile, lifted on her tiptoes to place her hands around his shoulders, one hand still holding her small bouquet.

"You've made me so happy," she whispered, and Antonio's fear melted away as his heart swelled with pride. All he wanted to do was keep the joyful light in her eyes, and know he'd caused it to be there, now and forever.

As Nakamura went to get the car, Antonio gripped Hana's hand. In the back seat, even when they reached his luxury hotel—the biggest, most glamorous international hotel in

Ginza—he never let go. As they walked into the hotel bar, which was sleekly black-and-white with high ceilings and modern art, the two of them were met with thunderous applause.

"Congratulations!" Emika Ito cried, holding up a champagne toast toward them. Stopping in the doorway, Antonio looked around in astonishment. Had everyone already heard about their wedding? But how?

The young woman continued, "The deal was lost, then it was struck. To the couple of the hour!"

Everyone applauded wildly, the entire Japan lead team, and the New York lawyers who'd been staying here the last few weeks to prep for the Iyokan deal. Emika had not been referring to their wedding, but the deal he'd actually forgotten about in all the excitement of marrying Hana.

He really was losing his mind...

Nestling close, Hana looked up at him with a blushing, intimate smile that he felt all over his body. Looking back at his employees, Antonio held up his hand for silence.

"Thank you to everyone who made this deal possible today. You will take CrossWorld Airways into not just Asia, but the future!" He paused to allow for applause, taking champagne from the tray of a passing waiter. Hana held her flute, but did not drink it. "But I have other news, even more important to me personally."

"What could be more important than business?" one of his lawyers hollered. Antonio smiled, then looked down at Hana in his arms.

"This wonderful woman, whom most of you know as my executive assistant, just became more. She's become, this very hour, my wife."

There was a gasp.

Hana looked up at him, biting her lip nervously. Antonio hesitated, wondering if he should hide the baby news for a few weeks more. But why? Half the people in the room had probably already guessed it, just based on the quickness of the marriage. Best to get all the juicy scandal out at once, and be done with it. "There's more." He paused. "We're expecting a baby."

The gasp became a roar, followed by more applause, as people surged forward to congratulate them, their faces all various degrees of shock and delight.

Hana was immediately circled by a group of women exclaiming over her and asking questions about the sudden wedding, and about her pregnancy. Antonio had a brief glimpse of her shy, happy smile as she was led away, before his view was blocked by one of his sharpest New York lawyers, coming forward with a well-cut suit and a big grin.

"I can't believe it, Mr. Delacruz! Here I thought you were immune!" The man shook his head, rolling his eyes heavenward as he held up his martini glass. "A toast to love! It gets the best of all of us, sooner or later!"

"We should toast marriage," a female lawyer chirped behind him. "Half our firm's billable hours come from divorce!" At the head lawyer's harsh glare, she blanched and mumbled, "Er, not that that will ever happen to you, Mr. Delacruz."

"Of course not." The head lawyer, a corporate shark whose going rate was three thousand dollars an hour, turned back to him with a blinding smile. "We've never handled Mr. Delacruz's personal matters. So tell me," he leaned forward confidentially, "Who did your prenup? I never heard a whisper. Tokyo's top firm, I assume." He gave a jovial laugh. "Obviously. It's not like you'd want to just *give away* half your company."

It hurt to hear those painful words out loud. Antonio flinched, feeling like he'd just been punched in the face, knocked out of his sensual dream into a harsh, cold reality.

Heart pounding, he slowly turned toward Hana. Across the room, she was smiling happily as she showed the other women the sparkling diamond on her finger. Then, suddenly, she looked up at the door, and her face lit up. With a gasp, she ran toward the door, her dark hair and pale pink sundress flying behind her.

Ren Tanaka stood in the doorway, his handsome face blank as he dropped his suitcase to the floor with a bang.

Watching as his wife threw her arms around the other man, Antonio felt suddenly sick inside.

He'd just given away his life, everything he cared about, everything that gave him value, to a woman who could now ruin him with a mere flick of her finger.

If Hana ever wanted to destroy Antonio, she could now. She could burn him to the ground. Leave him desolate and worthless and alone.

What had he just done?

"You're here!" Hana cried, throwing her arms around her best friend. "I didn't think you'd make it!"

"I didn't," Ren said grimly, pulling away from

her impulsive embrace. "I dropped everything and took the bullet train from Osaka. But I'm still too late."

She'd texted Ren her current location, after having left a long, rushed message on his phone hours before. She'd hoped and feared in equal parts that Ren would somehow make it to their wedding—hoped, because he was her only family, and feared, because she was afraid he'd try to talk her out of it or make a scene.

The truth was, Hana still couldn't quite believe she'd done it. She'd married Antonio.

But he'd offered her everything she'd ever wanted.

A home. A real father for their baby. Marriage. Passion.

And half the company. That was most shocking of all. Antonio—offering to share his airline?

For all this time, she'd told herself that a selfish playboy workaholic like Antonio Delacruz would never change.

But the truth was he already *had*. In the space of two days, he'd gone from rejecting her, to offering child support money, to asking her to be his mistress, to proposing marriage and asking to share full-time parenting.

Hana thought of what she'd learned about his heartbreaking childhood. And yet he was still willing to take the risk.

The more she learned about Antonio, the more she—cared.

And he was starting to care for her as well. He had to be. Because there was no other reason he would have offered to share his company.

If he was willing to share his most precious possession with her, didn't that also have to mean he'd be willing to truly share his life?

"How could you do it, Hana?" Ren demanded. "How could you marry him?"

Blinking, she looked at her friend in the elegant, crowded bar. His handsome face looked so strange. She said slowly, "Antonio is the father of my baby."

"And when I left Tokyo, you said you'd never see him again."

"He changed my mind."

"How?"

"He's not the man I thought he was, Ren. He wants to settle down, and be a father to our baby. Look, I know our wedding was a little sudden…"

"*Sudden.*" Ren's face looked grimmer still. "Is that what you call it?" He looked around the modern bar, filled with Antonio's employees and lawyers in their office clothes, getting drunk on martinis and sake. "This is your wedding reception?" He glanced at her pale pink sundress, which was starting to look a little limp after a full day of wear. "That's your wedding dress?"

She stiffened. "Do you really think I care about the wedding details?"

Ren stared at her, and she blanched as she remembered all the times as a girl that she'd described ridiculous dreams about her faraway, someday wedding.

Her throat suddenly hurt. A moment before, she'd convinced herself that their impulsive ceremony had been perfect. Efficient. No plans, no worries, just done and over with.

But now, it suddenly occurred to her that she'd never have another wedding. Or the chance to experience romantic, fairy-tale love.

Good, she told herself. So their child would never know how it felt to be excluded, as Hana had.

But the reassurance felt hollow.

"You don't even have a wedding cake," Ren said contemptuously, looking around. "Where are your seven tiers with white buttercream frosting flowers?"

"I don't care about cake." She lifted her hand defiantly. "Besides. He got me this."

Grabbing her hand, Ren closely examined the enormous platinum-set diamond ring. Then he snorted, releasing her hand. "That had to be his idea. Not yours."

Pulling back her arm, she said stiffly, "It doesn't matter. The wedding doesn't matter. Just the marriage. We're having a baby. We're a family now. Partners."

Silence fell between them, even as all around them people laughed over the bar's loud, raucous music. One of the New York lawyers was yelling, "A toast! To annual growth next year of eight percent!"

"Nine!" someone else roared, sloshing his drink.

Ren looked at her in the shadowy entrance of the bar.

"Partners," he said sardonically. "Very romantic."

Her cheeks heated. She couldn't meet his gaze. "You know I never asked for love."

"Yes," he said. "I know."

With an intake of breath, she looked up, and saw the blatant pain in Ren's dark eyes. Putting a hand to her mouth, she whispered, "I'm sorry.

I'm so sorry. It's so hideously unfair. I never meant to—"

"I know." He tried to smile. "I was stupid to let myself love you when I knew you wouldn't love me back. But I convinced myself—" He turned away. "It was stupid."

Hana felt grief that she'd hurt her best friend. And on the edges of that grief, she felt fear.

I was stupid to let myself love you when I knew you wouldn't love me back.

No, she told herself. She wouldn't let herself fall in love with Antonio. No matter how charming or wonderful her husband might be. Because no matter how much he'd changed, she knew he'd never love her back. That miracle would be a step too far.

But as she looked across the crowded room, she saw her husband sitting at the bar. He lifted his head and his dark eyes burned through her soul.

Taking a deep breath, Hana quickly turned away. "Please, Ren. Just be happy."

"Don't worry about me." His eyes narrowed. "But if your husband ever does the slightest thing to cause you pain—if he hurts you or disappoints you in any way—"

"He won't," Hana assured him. "Will you be all right?"

"I'll be fine."

"I never meant to—"

"Stop." A low strangled curse came from his throat. "I'll get over it, Hana."

"Get over it?"

He looked at her. "Loving you."

She'd never thought she could feel so sad, standing beside her best friend on what was supposed to be the happiest day of her life. Her view was suddenly blocked by Emika Ito.

"Congratulations again," she told Hana warmly. "Married, and expecting a baby!" She shook her head, grinning. "No one thought Mr. Delacruz would settle down. I've always heard you were an amazing person, Hana. Now I think you're a rock star!"

"Oh," said Hana, who didn't feel remotely rock star-ish at the moment.

Emika turned to Ren. "Mr. Delacruz wants to talk to you."

His eyes darkened. "He does?"

"Alone."

Antonio and Ren—talking alone? Anxiety ripped through Hana. "I'll come with you."

"No," he said.

"You don't have to do it—"

"You're wrong," Ren said grimly. He looked toward the bar. "I can hardly wait."

Glancing toward the doorway from where he was sitting, Antonio saw Ren Tanaka coming forward with a glower and turned back to the bartender. "Double scotch."

As the drink was placed in front of him, Antonio took a sip, letting the harsh liquid burn him from the inside. Scotch for a wedding reception. It should have been champagne, with toasts to the bridal couple, instead of to the future profitability of CrossWorld Airways. But then, as Antonio had told Hana, they weren't a normal couple.

No. Any normal man in his position would have insisted on a prenup, instead of stupidly offering up half his fortune.

He could trust Hana, he told himself. He could trust her. He did trust her.

Antonio pressed the glass against his forehead, to cool his hot skin.

"I hope you're proud of yourself." Tanaka's voice was cold as he slid into the empty bar stool beside him.

Turning, Antonio bared his teeth in a smile.

"If you mean proud of marrying Hana, then yes, I'm very proud. She's carrying my child and I've done right by her."

"*Right*," Tanaka sneered. He glanced back at Hana, who was still by the doorway talking to Emika Ito, throwing them worried glances. "The right thing would have been to set her free to marry someone who's worthy of her."

"That's you, I suppose."

"More than you'll ever be." Tanaka looked around. "This is how you marry Hana? No cake, no wedding dress, just some office party in a bar?"

The last thing Antonio needed was to be criticized just when he was already kicking himself about the prenup. His lip twisted in a snarl. "She doesn't love you, Tanaka. Get over it."

"She might have found a way to love me, someday, if you'd just left her alone. But you couldn't, could you? You selfishly took her for yourself."

"She kissed me first," Antonio took malicious pleasure in informing him. "I didn't seduce her. *She* kissed *me*."

The younger man's eyes flashed, then his jaw set. "You're a selfish bastard, Delacruz. You jump from one place and person to the next, because you're afraid if you stick around any-where too long, people will realize you're noth-ing. An empty husk."

From long practice, Antonio kept his expres-sion amused, so the other man wouldn't know he'd hit his target. His voice was cool as he pointed out, "And yet Hana still chose me over you."

"A choice you'll make her regret, won't you? Starting with this pathetic wedding."

"I've planned her an amazing honeymoon," said Antonio, who'd just that moment thought of it.

Tanaka muttered something in Japanese.

Antonio bared his teeth. "Consider your friendship with her over. Stay away from my wife."

"You'll never be good enough for her," the younger man replied coldly. "You know it. I know it." As the two men looked at Hana across the room, she turned and met Antonio's gaze. Almost at once, her stunning face lit up, and he unwillingly felt his heart rise. Then he heard Tanaka add under his breath, "And someday soon, Hana will know it, too."

CHAPTER EIGHT

HEAVEN. SHE WAS in heaven.

The hot Caribbean sun was shining on a sea that was so impossibly blue it burned Hana's eyes to look at it from the pink sand beach.

Looking out from the lounge chair beneath the open-air cabana, where she was stretched out in a turquoise string bikini, she lifted her sunglasses and watched her husband rise from the sea.

Rivulets of water ran from his dark hair down his thick neck and over the muscles and hollows of his torso, to the edge of his swim trunks. All that water, and as she looked at him, her mouth went dry.

Coming over to the cabana, which was just wooden pillars, a slatted roof and white curtains perched over the sand, Antonio smiled down at her, his eyes crinkling. "You should have joined me in the water."

"I was reading…" Then she saw that her book

had fallen from her lap, and lay upside down in the sand, and blushed. His smile widened, and he sat beside her on the lounge chair.

"I have other ways to entertain you," he said softly, running his large hand from her neck down the valley between her breasts, to her belly, naked and warmed by the sun. Her breathing quickened.

Her husband. Antonio was her husband now. She still couldn't quite believe it. When they'd left their reception in Tokyo, he'd surprised her by taking her on a honeymoon to his private island in the Caribbean, where she knew for a fact he'd never taken anyone. It had always been his private demesne, where he went to get away from the world.

But he'd brought her here.

"You're so good to me," she said.

"So you don't mind not having the wedding of your dreams?"

Not for the first time, Hana wondered what Ren had said to him in Tokyo. The last thing she wanted was for Antonio to feel bad. "I didn't need a romantic wedding."

Antonio gave her a skeptical look.

"Well, the honeymoon has more than made up for it," she said, sighing with pleasure as she leaned back on the lounge chair, and that, at least, was utterly true.

After three days on his private island, she felt deliciously good all over. It was the longest vacation either of them had ever had. With their phones turned off and the company's decisions temporarily delegated to the COO, there had been nothing for them to do but enjoy each other.

Instead of thinking about work, they'd spent their days making love. Staying in a luxurious, sprawling villa, cared for by a live-in staff of ten, they'd laughed, splashing on the beach, kissing in the shallow blue water, drinking virgin piña coladas and eating seafood brought fresh from the sea.

"You look tense," her husband informed her now with a wicked smile. "Let me give you a massage."

Hana shivered as he slowly ran his hands down the length of her bare legs. As she felt his fingers caress and stroke the hollows of her feet, her gaze traced dreamily over the satin smoothness of her husband's powerful body. His muscular thighs, his flat belly. His thick forearms, laced with dark hair. The hard line of his cheekbones and jaw, shadowed with bristle. His cruelly sensual lips.

Dappled sunlight flashed through the slatted roof of the cabana. A warm fragrant breeze, scented of sea salt and lush tropical flowers, caressed her skin, blowing against the gauzy white curtains that protected them from the eyes of the villa's well-trained, discreet staff.

This cabana had become one of her favorite places on the private island, on the edge of the pink sand beach, with a breathtaking view of the Caribbean, separated from the bright blue horizon only by the sweep of green palm trees across the cove. And she'd never loved it more than now, on their last precious day before they returned to Madrid.

Antonio's hands stopped, and his dark eyes seared hers.

"I want you, *querida*," he growled.

She caught her breath. In spite of the hours he'd spent making love to her day and night since they'd arrived at this island, she wanted him as badly as if they'd never even kissed, as if she weren't already carrying his baby inside her.

How was it possible that each time they made love, instead of satiating their desire, it only caused their fire to burn hotter?

Sitting up in the lounge chair, she reached out to stroke his rough cheek. His dark hair, still wet and plastered back, revealed the scar on his left temple where the awful boys at a Spanish orphanage had once beaten a six-year-old boy for crying. Gently, deliberately, she ran her fingertips over the raised scar.

With an intake of breath, he caught her wrist.

"Kintsugi," she whispered.

His eyes widened. "What?"

Pulling her wrist from his grasp, she explained, "It's a Japanese art, when broken pottery is rejoined by molten gold. But it's more than that. It means something broken and repaired is more precious and beautiful than something unused and whole." Her eyes met his. "It shows history. It shows life."

He gave a low, rueful laugh. "Oh, Hana," he said softly. "You make the world new. I wish you could always look at me the way you are now."

"I will." She ran her hand slowly down his bare, warm chest, still traced with droplets of water from his dripping wet hair, feeling the softness of his skin over his hard muscles.

Tensing, Antonio looked toward the sea. "Tanaka—"

Her hand froze. "What did Ren say to you?"

"It doesn't matter." He looked back at her. "I don't want you to see him again."

"How can you say that? He's my friend."

"And you're my wife."

She drew away, the good feelings lost. "You're being ridiculous."

But as she started to rise to her feet, he pulled her back. "Fine. We won't waste our honeymoon talking about Tanaka." Running his hand down her naked belly, he slowly lowered his lips to hers. "I have something more fun in mind, anyway…"

Any further discussion was impossible as he kissed her. But his lips were barely on hers before there was a wrench below them, as the lounge chair cracked under their mutual weight. At lightning speed, Antonio was on his feet, catching her in his arms.

Held protectively against his bare chest, she looked at him in amazement. "How did you do that?"

"I'll never let you fall." He gently lowered her to her feet in front of him, their skin touching, his arms still around her waist.

Behind his handsome face, edged with wild dark hair, she saw the bright blue Caribbean. She felt the warm breezes off the sea.

And she felt it again, her heart swelling inside her as she'd never felt before, rising until she felt like she was nothing but heart, through muscle and bone, to the very edge of her skin. It terrified her.

She was falling in love with her husband.

Every time he made love to her, every time they talked and laughed together, every time he looked at her the way he was looking at her now, she fell a little deeper.

She heard herself say in a small voice, "You won't?"

"Never," he whispered. Gently, he lifted her chin, smoothing back long dark tendrils of her hair. "I'm your partner. In bed." He kissed her cheeks. "In business." He kissed down between her full breasts, letting the tip of his tongue taste with a flick a tiny bead of sweat. "In life."

Her knees went weak as she staggered back a single step, bracing herself against a thick wooden post on the edge of the large cabana.

"I trust you," he said. Something in his dark eyes made her wonder if he was speaking to her, or to himself. There was something he wasn't telling her. Some hidden fear.

But as her lips parted to ask, he fell to his knees on the sand in front of her. Leaning forward, he tenderly kissed the bare skin of her pregnant belly before he looked up past the full breasts straining the bikini top, to her luminous eyes.

"Forever," he murmured.

Hana looked down at him. She heard the soft roar of the sea against the shore, the birds soaring through the palm trees above. She felt hot, trembling all over.

Silently, he reached around her back and loosened the tie of her bikini top, letting it fall to the sand. He cupped her breasts with his large hands. Leaning forward, he gently suckled a pink nipple, swirling it with his tongue, making her gasp before he moved to the other.

Still kneeling on the sand, he stroked down her waist to her hips, then undid the ties of her string bikini bottom, and that, too, fell to the sand.

He leaned forward, lifting one of her knees over his shoulder. He breathed in the scent of her, then kissed her there, between her naked thighs.

Holding her breath, she looked down at him kneeling between her tanned legs. Behind him, the gauzy white curtains shielding the cabana blew softly in the breeze, as flashes of golden light stroked patterns on his skin.

He lowered his head between her legs and tasted her, making her shudder with desire. Gripping her hips with his hands, with one of her legs still tossed over his shoulder, he licked and suckled her most secret places, until she began to shake, gripping her hands on the wooden pillar behind her as she cried out.

He rose to his feet, and yanked off his swim trunks almost violently, the hard shaft jutting from his body. Grasping her backside, he lifted her off the ground, pulling her legs to wrap around his hips. Leaning her against the pillar, he pushed slowly inside her, filling her inch by inch. She gasped, straining against him as he stretched her to the limit. He thrust again, and again, increasing the rhythm until he rode her, hard and deep. Panting for breath, she felt the world spinning around her, in Caribbean blue and pink sand and green palm trees, and at the center of it all, the man she…

The man she…

Tension twisted inside her, higher and higher, until her body shattered into a million pieces.

Across the beach, the seagulls echoed her cry, and with one last thrust, he roared as he exploded inside her.

Slowly, she came back to earth. She lowered her feet once more to the sand. Her husband held her, the two of them naked together in the cabana on the private pink sand beach. And he tenderly kissed her.

But as she pressed her cheek against his chest, her heart was pounding at what she could no longer deny.

She was in love with her husband.

It's all right, Hana told herself desperately. It'll be all right.

"You're crying, *querida*," Antonio said, touching her cheek. He gave a sudden wicked smile. "Am I just that good?"

"Yes," she managed. "You're just that good."

And she tried not to think about how he'd told her from the beginning he wasn't capable of loving anyone. She tried not to remember the pain in Ren's words. *I was stupid to let myself love you when I knew you wouldn't love me back.*

And Hana felt a cold hollow in her belly.

Happiness suffused Antonio's body as he held his wife in the beachside cabana, the two of them still standing naked in each other's arms. She was everything to him, he thought drowsily, playing with the ends of her long dark hair. Everything.

Then his eyes opened as he stared past her, out at the sea.

Yes, she was everything. She owned him now. Half of him. Half this island. Half this villa. Half his company. Half his soul. She could cut him right in half, anytime she chose. Cut him in half and just walk away—

You'll never be good enough for her. You know it. I know it. And soon, Hana will know it, too.

How long would it be before she realized Antonio was utterly unworthy of her? How long before she saw the deep, mysterious flaw that had caused everyone, starting with his own parents, to steer clear of him?

Kintsugi, indeed. Nothing broken was ever better than something unused and whole, he thought bitterly. No philosophy would ever make him believe otherwise. Not against the experience of his life.

Antonio tried to fight the panic rising inside him. He repeated to himself, over and over, that he could trust Hana. Hadn't she proved that, time and time again?

He trusted her. He trusted her. He repeated the words like a spell of protection. Hana alone had never lied to him, never betrayed him. He could trust her, he told himself. He could trust her. He had no choice.

But what if he couldn't? What if she left—and

took everything, leaving him utterly destroyed? How could he just stand by and wait for it to happen?

CHAPTER NINE

HANA WASN'T SURE how it started, or why.

The week they were married was the happiest of her life. But every day after that, there was a little less happiness, like air let out of a leaky tire.

For the last six months, they'd lived as husband and wife in Madrid, working each day in the CrossWorld Airways headquarters, a glass and steel skyscraper in the financial center of the city, then sleeping together each night in the gorgeous bedroom of their nineteenth-century *palacio*, with its wrought-iron veranda covered with bright pink bougainvillea.

Their lives should have been perfect. And they were—on the outside.

But on the inside…

She still didn't understand what had happened. All summer, from the moment she'd married him in Tokyo last April, she should have felt like the luckiest woman on earth. So, except for the happy day in June when they'd found out they were having a daughter, why did it feel like each day, she had less than the day before?

Like now. Coming to tell her husband it was time to leave for the party, Hana froze in the hallway as she heard the COO's voice carry through the partially open door of Antonio's office.

"I understand Señora Delacruz isn't getting paid. She doesn't even have a title. Why?"

"I haven't decided yet what my wife's place should be." Antonio's voice was cold.

"You could add her to the board. Even as chairman." The man gave a low laugh. "You must know CrossWorld couldn't do without her."

"I know." Her husband's voice became colder still. "She is very popular with the staff."

"Popular with everyone… But it's awkward, since no one is quite sure what her official position is. It makes it confusing. Does she have a position here, or not?"

Hana strained to listen. She'd asked Antonio so many times over the summer when he would be making her new position in the company official, and giving her some title beyond just being his wife. But every time she asked, his expression closed up. "Later," he always said. And that was exactly what he said now.

"Later. We have more important things to discuss." Antonio paused. "Like how we can gain control of Lund Avionics..."

With an intake of breath, Hana abruptly pushed inside his door. "No. You can't take the poor man's company! It would be unthinkably cruel."

Her husband glowered at her. Looking around his sleek office with its beautiful view of Madrid, she saw not just the COO, but also his secretary and the head of acquisitions, all of whom were gaping at Hana now.

Antonio didn't like employees arguing with him, so they rarely did. Maybe that was why the COO, and everyone else at the Madrid headquarters, appreciated Hana. As his secretary, she'd been the only one to push back against Antonio, even gently. Now, as his wife and partner, she did it full bore.

She didn't hold back. She couldn't be afraid to argue for what she thought was right for the company. It was their family's airline, after all, that would someday be run by their daughter.

So now, in response to Antonio's furious glare, Hana coolly lifted her chin.

Let others be yes-men and toadies. She was his wife. This company was half hers, even if she didn't yet officially have the title or shares to prove it.

Once, her job had been to make him look good. Now, it was to be fearless enough to point out when he was wrong.

As he was now.

"Lund Avionics is one of our core suppliers," she said firmly.

His black eyes glittered. "Exactly why we should acquire it. They're vulnerable to a hostile takeover right now."

"Vertical integration doesn't make sense in this case." She glared at him. "Plus, I don't like kicking someone when they're down."

Antonio folded his arms, pulling up his tall, powerful frame in his sophisticated suit. "It's already decided."

"I know it is." Folding her arms over her hugely pregnant belly, she matched him toe to toe. "We're not doing it."

The others in the room looked back and forth between them, wide-eyed, as if they were at a tennis match.

Antonio narrowed his eyes as if he hated her.

And for the first time since they'd returned to Madrid, Hana felt shaken.

He abruptly turned away, speaking to the COO and VP of acquisitions on other topics before dismissing them a few minutes later. The COO paused, looking at Hana as he left.

"Nice work lining up the New York union negotiations, Señora Delacruz."

"I just wish I could be part of the negotiating team," she said ruefully. Antonio had convinced her it would be unwise, this close to her due date, to travel to New York for a week of stressful, contentious negotiations with the employees union.

"I do, too. You have a magic touch with employees. With customers and suppliers, too. And your new charity initiative—genius! Which reminds me." The man looked at his watch. "My wife will have my hide if I don't head home to get ready."

"We need to do the same." But as Hana glanced at her husband, her shy smile fell away. Antonio looked so strange, almost green. As if he'd just been kicked in the teeth. She didn't understand. "Antonio?"

"Yes," he said tersely, not looking at her. "We should go."

But as the chauffeur drove the two of them home through the streets of Madrid, her husband barely looked at her.

Hana was at a loss. Surely he couldn't be upset at her for making her mark at their company? Or for having a different opinion, when they were both simply trying to do right by everyone?

Whatever the reason was, from the moment they'd returned to Madrid, to the place she'd thought would be her forever home, Antonio had seemed more cold and distant each day.

Could he have somehow learned her secret? Glancing at him again in the back of the Bentley, Hana took a deep breath. Was it possible he was actually trying to drive her away, as he'd done with all his mistresses before?

But she wasn't a mistress. She was his wife.

So why? When had Antonio started to pull away from her? Had it been on their honeymoon? She tried to remember. The Caribbean sun had been spun gold on the pink sand beach. For four days, she and Antonio had splashed in the sea and made love. A blush suffused Hana's cheeks as she remembered that time in the cabana, when he'd lifted her legs around his hips as he'd plunged into her, riding her hard.

That would be impossible now. Her belly had

grown in the last six months. With only a few weeks until her due date now, she was huge. The Spanish summer had nearly melted her with heat. Thank heavens that finally, in late September, the autumn air had grown cooler.

But the nights were hotter than ever, at least in their bedroom. Sex wasn't their problem. Antonio seemed to think it was his duty to bring her to explosive, gasping fulfillment at least twice a night. Last night, he'd done it three times.

It had become harder and harder for Hana to hide her feelings. Since their honeymoon, she'd buried her love for him deep in her heart. She tried to forget. She couldn't risk him knowing. Because if he couldn't return her love, he'd scorn her, or worse—pity her.

What would she do then? Could she still bear to be his wife, to live by his side, to sleep in his bed, if she knew for certain he'd never feel anything for her beyond friendship?

No. She wouldn't break up their family and home, just because her husband didn't love her back. Home and stability were far more important than love.

Weren't they?

The crowded city streets of Madrid in the early evening rush hour were flooded with the last rays of autumn sunshine as they went home. They were running late for their own party. But Hana could barely think about the charity ball that had been her project for the last two months. She kept giving Antonio side glances in the back of the Bentley, as, in the front seat, Ramon Garcia kept up a stream of affable chatter in Spanish with the chauffeur.

Antonio pressed the button to slide up the privacy screen.

"I didn't appreciate you contradicting me in front of the staff."

Antonio's voice was terse in the seat beside her. Her hands tightened in her lap.

"You mean about the avionics deal? I just don't think it's right to take advantage of the poor guy's divorce, that's all."

"If we don't take advantage of it, someone else will." His expression was hard. "And his liquidity problems are his own fault, for not making his wife sign a prenup."

"Don't be too hard on him. After all," Hana tilted her head with a flirtatious smile, trying to lighten the mood, "you didn't make *me* sign one…"

His dark eyes were grim. "That's something I've been meaning to discuss with you."

The smile slid from Hana's face. "You want me to sign a prenup?"

"A postnuptial agreement, yes." Antonio looked calmly handsome in his perfectly tailored dark suit. "And perhaps you should stop coming to the office."

Hana's jaw dropped. "You're kicking me out?"

"Nothing so dramatic," Antonio said gruffly. "It's just that you're about to become a mother..."

"You're about to become a father, but I don't hear anything about *you* leaving your job."

"Our baby will be so tiny," he persisted. "Helpless. Surely you would not wish to abandon a newborn to the care of nannies."

His words felt like an attack. Like he was trying to give her an argument that she could not fight, rather than tell her his real reasons. "I'm planning to stay home for a while, yes. But CrossWorld Airways is part of our family. Even the name comes from our surname. In a few months, I'll return to work and bring the baby with me."

"It's an office, not a nursery," he said coldly.

"Why are you acting like this?" Hana glared at him. "Just because I didn't want us to buy that poor man's company at fire sale prices?"

"Since you mention it, I think it does confuse

some of my employees when you give orders, since you don't have an official position at the company."

"I'm your equal partner," she said.

He said nothing.

Searching his closed face, she pressed, "I am, aren't I?"

"The post-nup is fairly standard." Antonio suddenly wouldn't meet her eyes. "It just says, in case of a split, we'll each keep the assets we came into the marriage with. You also get a generous settlement, of course."

The passing streets of Madrid seemed to whirl in front of her eyes. "You...you don't want to share the company with me."

"Don't say it like that."

"Like what?"

"Accusingly," he accused.

Hana stared at him.

After all his fine words about wanting their airline to be a family company, he was going to go back on his word and keep it for himself alone?

The foundation of everything she'd believed about their marriage shifted beneath her.

"You lied to me?"

"I've reassessed the situation."

"You said the company was ours," she said. "That we'd share it, and build it together for our child."

Antonio looked at her emotionlessly in the back seat of the car. "You're not the one who created an empire from nothing. It's mine. I built it. All you did was help me a little."

Turning, Hana stared blindly in front of her, at the blank privacy screen. She felt the soft calf-skin leather of the Bentley's leather seat beneath her fingers.

"Then..." Hana looked down at her swelling belly. She said in a low voice, "By that argument, our daughter is only mine."

Antonio glared at her. "That's not fair, and you know it."

"Fair?" Hana thought of all her effort and love she'd put into CrossWorld Airways over the last two and a half years, working every bit as long and hard as Antonio had. And for the last six months, she'd done it without salary or title. She'd done it for love. Because she'd thought they were building something. As a couple. As a *family*.

No wonder she'd felt a growing emotional distance between them. She was the only one who'd even thought they were a team. The lump in her throat turned to a razor blade.

"Did you ever intend to share it with me?" she choked out. "Or was it just a ploy to make me marry you?"

Looking at her evenly, Antonio countered, "Is that the only reason you married me? Because you wanted to get your hands on half my company?" He shook his head furiously. "I never dreamed you'd challenge me at every step, luring the staff to your side, trying to take it from me like this!"

"I'm not!"

"Then what are you doing?"

Staring at him as the car stopped, she whispered, "Trying to make it better."

She dimly saw the *palacio* ahead on their elegant, tree-lined street. As the Bentley paused, waiting to turn into the gated driveway that led into the *palacio*'s courtyard, Antonio suddenly narrowed his eyes, trying to see through the window. He pressed another button and spoke through the car's intercom. "What is it, Carlos?"

"I'm not sure, *señor*," the driver responded. "Someone is blocking the gate."

Hana didn't understand how her husband could be talking about the stupid gate, when he'd just ripped out her heart. "What made you like this?"

"Like what?" Antonio bit out, turning back to her.

"Suspicious. Cruel!"

"Experience," he said coldly, and got out of the car.

Hana blinked, feeling sick and shivering in her maternity suit. For months, she'd been excited about tonight's fund-raiser ball, the kickoff of the new charity initiative she'd created for the company. She'd spent weeks choosing an exquisite gown from one of the top designers in Madrid. She'd never worn a dress so fancy in her life. It was fit for a princess, far more glamorous and fairy-tale-like than the simple pink sundress that had been her wedding dress. She'd been so excited for Antonio to see her in it. In spite of being so pregnant, she'd dreamed of a romantic night, of him taking her in his arms on the dance floor. *I love you,* querida. *I never realized it till this very moment. My heart is yours, now and forever.* And it was then, only then, that she could confess her love.

Stupid dream!

Instead, they'd have to pretend to be a happy couple in front of all their high-powered guests, so the share price of CrossWorld Airways didn't drop at rumors of a potential marital split. The stock market was ruthless. The party was due to start in an hour, and she still had to take a shower and get ready.

"Something's happening at the gate," their bodyguard said, getting out of the car. "Stay here, Señora Delacruz."

At the guarded gate at the end of the tall, wrought-iron fence, Hana saw her husband approaching a strange man with his back toward them, arguing with their security guard.

Getting out of the car over the driver's protests, she followed Antonio and their bodyguard past the privacy hedges toward their *palacio*'s gatehouse.

Could it be Ren? she thought with sudden longing. She hadn't spoken to her friend since the wedding. She'd tried, but he hadn't returned any of her messages. Could Ren have come to Madrid after all this time to say he was ready to be friends again?

Then the man's hat fell off, and she saw he was a white-haired stranger, nothing like Ren at all.

"If you don't leave, I'll call the police..." the security guard was saying in Spanish, glaring at the stranger.

"But if you'll just give him this letter…" Then the elderly man saw Antonio, and his face lit up with relief. "Señor Delacruz. It is you, is it not? I've seen you in the newspaper."

Antonio glowered at him. "Who are you?"

"Please—this is for you." The old man held out a white envelope. Antonio didn't take it.

"Back away." Ramon Garcia held up a brawny arm to ward off the elderly stranger.

Why such a fuss? In another moment, they'd be calling for police with sirens blazing. And all for an old man who just wanted to give Antonio something.

"What do you want, *señor*?" Hana asked him kindly.

The man straightened. His eyes were rheumy and red, and in spite of his carefully pressed, if outdated, coat and trousers, he smelled of wine. But he still had a strange dignity as he held out a small white envelope. "Please, *señora*."

"Don't take it," Garcia warned, but she ignored him. She took the envelope.

"Bless you," the elderly man whispered. "She doesn't have long. I couldn't let her life end like this."

"What are you talking about?" Hana said, alarmed. "Who are you?"

"I'm Dr. Mendoza from Etxetarri, to the north." He slowly looked at Antonio. "I delivered you when you were born."

Antonio's jaw dropped. It would have been hilarious to see him so surprised, if Hana hadn't felt the same shock.

The doctor's rheumy eyes fell as his shoulders sagged. He whispered, "Then I took you south to Andalusia, and left you in a basket."

Hana caught her breath. No one knew that story—no one. Glancing at her husband, she waited for him to say something, anything. When he did not move, she said anxiously to the man, "Please, come inside." What did the charity ball matter, compared to this? "We have so many questions..."

Shaking his head, he looked back at Antonio. "Your mother is dying. You must go to her—"

"Get off my property," Antonio said grimly. "Now."

"Antonio!" Hana cried, scandalized.

"Read the letter," the man pleaded. "Before it's too late."

Turning, he shuffled away, his gait uneven.

"My apologies, *señor*," the gate guard said to Antonio, hanging his head.

"You should have called the police immediately," Garcia reprimanded him, then turned to Hana. "*Señora*, give me the envelope."

"Why?" she said, still watching the elderly man disappear down the street.

"I'll dispose of it. Have it tested for anthrax, poisons, blackmail attempts, then thrown away."

"How can you be so suspicious and rude?" Her eyes snapped to her husband. "And you!"

Antonio didn't even look at her. Without a word, he turned on his heel and walked through the gate toward the *palacio.*

Still gripping the letter, she hurried after him.

Inside the courtyard, a steady stream of caterers and florists carried canapés and flower arrangements into the elegant, nineteenth-century palace, constructed of limestone in the classical style. It was difficult to keep up with his stride, so she increased her pace as much as a heavily pregnant woman could. It was almost as if Antonio didn't *want* her to catch up.

Inside the *palacio*'s grand foyer, with its soaring ceiling and dazzling chandelier, she saw Manuelita, the housekeeper, directing traffic. "You're back!" the older woman said, beaming at her. Hana and Manuelita had been friends for years, since she'd only been a secretary. The woman was almost like a mother to her, or at the very least an aunt. "There are some questions about the music—"

"I'm sorry, it will have to wait," Hana called, hurrying after Antonio, who was already disappearing down the long hall, past the antique suit of armor, toward the stained glass window. When she finally caught up with him in the study, she was panting for breath.

"Antonio!" she said accusingly.

Plantation shutters blocked the sunlight, leaving her husband's face in shadow as he looked up calmly from his dark wood desk. "Yes?"

"This letter!" Holding it out anxiously, she went to the desk. The room was masculine and dark, with bookshelves and leather furniture. A fire crackled in the fireplace. "Don't you want to rip it open?"

He leaned back in his chair. "Not particularly."

"Are you kidding?" She looked down at the envelope. Antonio's name was written on it in spidery, uncertain handwriting. "But you've wanted to know about your past all your life!"

"Maybe once I did. Now I really don't care." Tenting his fingers on the desk, he curled his lip. "And the man hardly seemed credible. I smelled alcohol on him from ten feet away."

"Just open it!" She dropped the envelope on

the desk in front of him. When he didn't move, she tilted her head challengingly. "Unless you're afraid."

His forehead furrowed as he stared down at the envelope. He picked it up.

Then, without reading, he abruptly crumpled it into a ball. "It is nothing."

"You didn't even open it!"

"I am wealthy. I am known." He rose to his feet. "There are always crackpots who want to cause trouble, who scheme to get money."

"But he didn't ask for money. You heard him. He said he left you in a basket as a baby. Who even knows about that?"

His expression was hard as granite. "I've heard enough." He went grimly toward the fireplace.

"Wait," Hana said, alarmed, "you're not going to—?"

She gasped as Antonio tossed the crumpled ball into the fire.

"How could you?" she whispered, staring at the envelope, as the spidery handwriting burned. "You don't even want to know the reason your parents abandoned you?"

"I don't give a damn."

"I would give anything to have my parents or grandmother back. To have family." Her voice became shrill. "Your parents might be alive and you don't want to know? You won't even give them a chance to explain?"

"No." His voice was cold.

"Why?"

"If my parents showed up begging on their knees, I still wouldn't speak to them. They made their choice. The doctor, if that's really what he was, made his choice, as well." He lifted his chin. "Let them all live with it."

"But—"

"Never speak to me of this again." Going back to his desk, Antonio opened a briefcase and held out a stack of papers.

"What's this?"

"The postnuptial agreement," he said coolly. "Read and sign it before I leave for New York tomorrow. Tonight, if possible." Antonio gave a cold smile, his black eyes icy as a January night. "I'm going to get ready for the party."

And he left.

Holding the post-nup in her numb hands, Hana stared at the open doorway, in shock over what she'd learned in the last hour.

Her husband had betrayed her. She thought he'd changed, but he'd never had any intention of sharing either his company or his life with her. And she knew, if she wasn't at the office, they'd lead separate lives. He routinely worked sixteen-hour days. How could he possibly be a real father? A real husband?

He hadn't changed. He still wouldn't let anyone have the slightest control over his life, or his heart.

Perhaps his heart had been broken by his parents' desertion, the day he was born. But Antonio wasn't even interested in trying to heal or learning to trust again. He preferred to continue living as he was—with a cold heart, and an iron grip on his company and fortune. Their only real connection was when he made love to her so passionately at night. But how long could Hana continue to share her body with him, after he'd betrayed his promise to her that they would be equal partners and share their lives?

If she stayed with him, she would be his possession. His servant, almost. Servicing him in bed, running his home, raising his child.

If she stayed?

She looked around the house she'd dreamed could be her home, then down at the postnuptial agreement in her hands. *In case of a split,* he'd said.

There was only one play she had left. One

last chance to see if she could convince him to change, to heal his heart. What did she have to lose now by taking the risk? Hana crushed the papers to her chest.

Nothing. Nothing at all.

CHAPTER TEN

ANTONIO PACED IMPATIENTLY at the bottom of the *palacio*'s sweeping staircase.

An hour. An hour since he'd left her in his study and told her to get ready. It wasn't like Hana to be late. But apparently that had changed. Just as it once hadn't been like her to attack or purposefully provoke him. But that, too, had become a habit with her lately.

At first, working with her had been good, just like when she was his secretary. All summer, they'd shared the thrill of closing the deals that gave CrossWorld Airways the routes they needed for exponential growth. First had been Tokyo, then Rio, then Nairobi. Tomorrow, he'd leave for New York to deal with the union. Once he built out North America, it would be the final piece of the puzzle.

But over the summer, Hana had changed. She'd started to flaunt her growing influence. Which was a problem. Because while Antonio's employees respected and feared him for his vision, hard work and ruthlessness, they *loved* Hana.

He didn't understand why she'd changed, when she'd never once tried to work against him before. Gaining the loyalty of his company's leadership team! Contradicting Antonio's orders!

Hearing her defy his decisions in front of his staff that morning, after the COO had actually demanded for Hana to be on the board— as chairman, second only to Antonio's status as CEO!—had been the final straw. He'd known he had to get her out of the company for good. It was bad enough that she already had so much power over him as his wife and the mother of his child. He couldn't let her seize the leadership of his company from him, along with everything else.

He'd been insane to ever offer to share his airline with her. He'd been out of his mind at the time, desperate to convince her to marry him. But he'd never imagined Hana could act like this, trying to seize control, to push Antonio out of the company he'd built with his bare hands. Without the company, who was he?

No one.

Well, he'd come to his senses. Hana would

sign the post-nup. He didn't truly believe she wanted to lead the company. He didn't know why she'd become so focused on business. What she really wanted was a home and family. How many times had she said it? And that was what he'd given her. He'd kept the headquarters in Madrid because she wanted to live here, where she'd made friends. He would be glad for her to run her new charity initiative, as long as she stopped trying to run his company.

So why was she late for her own fund-raiser? Antonio straightened in his well-cut tuxedo, gritting his teeth as he looked up the staircase. Did she expect him to greet their guests alone?

Stopping his pacing, he scowled, narrowing his eyes. His hands tightened at his sides. Perhaps she'd gotten distracted listening to a staff member's problems. Her caring heart left her an easy mark. Like the way she hadn't wanted to do a hostile takeover of Lund Avionics, because it was "unthinkably cruel." Or how she'd fallen for the story of the elderly so-called doctor who'd dropped off that ridiculous letter claiming to be the truth about Antonio's parents. He scowled. He'd barely picked up the envelope before his hands had started shaking so hard he'd known there was only one thing to do—destroy it.

Just open it. Unless you're afraid.

He couldn't believe Hana would ambush him that way. Why would she ever think he'd want to open some crackpot's letter?

There'd been no reason for him to read it. Either the old man had been lying, in which case reading it was a waste of his time, or else he was telling the truth—in which case, Antonio *really* didn't want to read it. If the parents who'd cold-bloodedly abandoned him as a newborn suddenly wanted to worm their way back into his life now they'd discovered he was rich, Antonio wanted no part of it.

Let them suffer with the knowledge that the baby they'd thrown away could have made their fortune. He'd turned out to have some worth, after all. And they'd blown it.

He had a new family now. A beautiful wife here at home, raising their child, supporting him while he built his empire alone.

His heartbeat slowed to normal pace. He looked at his platinum watch. Guests had already started to arrive in the ballroom, without either host or hostess to greet them. Where was Hana? This was her party, damn it!

"Antonio."

Hearing his wife's soft voice calling from above, he looked up, and his jaw dropped.

There at the top of the sweeping staircase, he saw a princess.

Hana's long dark hair had been twisted into a ballerina bun at the top of her head, surrounded by a delicate diamond tiara. She was wearing a blue gown, cut Regency-style, with a very low bodice that showcased a diamond and sapphire necklace, as well as her overflowing breasts. Layers of baby blue fabric skimmed lightly over her full, pregnant belly, and she wore white gloves that went up past her elbows.

Her brown eyes were guarded as she came down the staircase, her gloved hand skimming over the handrail, floating so lightly that he looked at her feet to see if she were being carried by doves, or at least glass slippers. No, just stiletto sandals in matching baby blue.

"You look stunning," he said when she reached the bottom of the stairs.

She smiled, but it seemed strangely sad. Why? Because he'd informed her he wouldn't give her half the company? No, that couldn't be it. Hana was no gold digger. All along, she'd wanted to focus on their family and home. He was simply helping her do that.

But in this moment, she looked so glamorous he almost couldn't recognize her. Hana's lips were full and red, her brown eyes rich and expressive beneath the extravagant sweep of dark lashes.

She paused. "I read the post-nup."

"And signed it?"

"And...we'll talk about it later."

"You will sign," Antonio said, holding out his arm. He knew it was the only way they could both be happy.

Lowering her gaze, she gently placed her gloved hand around the arm of his black tuxedo jacket. "Shall we greet our guests?"

As they entered the *palacio*'s ballroom, Antonio saw it had been transformed. The gilded mirrors were now covered with red roses, like a romantic fantasy.

Strange. He'd owned this *palacio* for a decade. He'd bought it as a symbol of how far he'd come, a way to prove to everyone, especially himself, that he was no longer a scruffy orphan, a pathetic squalling foundling who'd had to be given a name by the shocked nuns at a church.

This palace had been commissioned in the early nineteenth century by a young nobleman who'd come to a bad end in a duel, dying for

HER BOSS'S ONE-NIGHT BABY

love, "which," Antonio always finished smugly when he'd told the story, "shows he was too stupid to deserve such a magnificent home." It had taken several years of remodeling to bring the palace into the current century, with modern comforts and technology.

But Antonio had left this ballroom almost intact, from the gilded mirrors to the vibrant frescoes of Cupid and amorous couples on the ceiling. The ballroom had seemed a useless anachronism, so ridiculously romantic he'd never bothered with it. And it had never been more romantic than now, covered with flowers and filled with guests in tuxedos and ball gowns.

But somehow, he didn't hate it.

Antonio looked at his regally beautiful wife on his arm, listening as she greeted each guest courteously and intelligently, thanking them for attending CrossWorld Airways's charity fundraiser in several different languages. He felt a swell of pride.

The evening passed in a swirl of conversation and laughter, with three hundred people in the ballroom all charmed by his wife, unable to resist her sweet pleas that they should donate to the CrossWorld Kids charity, which in addition to raising funds for medicine and supplies would offer free transport to medical teams. As she told heartfelt stories of the good that could be done, he was mesmerized by her beautiful face and the tremble of her voice. He congratulated himself on marrying her.

Antonio felt strangely reluctant to leave her side during the ball. He was irritated when he was interrupted by Horace Lund, the recently divorced owner of the American avionics firm that had lately become a takeover target, the same company Hana had pleaded with him to leave alone. But how could he, when Lund Avionics was so ripe for the taking?

As the pudgy, sweaty, anxious man pulled him into a quiet corner of the ballroom, Antonio gritted his teeth. "What do you want?"

He braced himself, wondering if the man would burst into sobs and beg for money. Maybe he should call security before Lund ruined the whole charity ball.

Horace Lund took a deep breath, then said unhappily, "I want you to buy my company."

Antonio's jaw dropped, then he caught himself. "Because you know I will take it, whether you wish it or not."

"My company is a picked-over bone being

fought over by dogs. And there's no way I can consolidate our debts, not in the middle of this divorce." The middle-aged man wiped his eyes. "I'd rather sell my company to you whole than risk another corporation getting it. At least I know you won't break my company up for parts and fire all our employees." He took a deep breath. "As long as my employees still have jobs…"

The older man cut a pitiable figure. Antonio discovered he felt sorry for him. But why should he? The man had done it to himself. Lund had been an idiot for not asking his wife for a prenup before she divorced him. Just being around the sad, hunched man made Antonio feel edgy. It made him more determined than ever to make Hana sign the papers tonight, no matter how proud of her he was in this moment.

He looked back at Hana, glowing onstage as she spoke so earnestly about CrossWorld's new charity. He remembered her voice. *Plus, I don't like kicking someone when they're down.*

"No," he heard himself say suddenly. "I won't buy it."

"You're going to let the other airline take it?" The other man's eyes filled with fear. "They're heartless. They'll fire everyone—"

"I'm offering you a loan, Lund," he said abruptly. "On reasonable terms."

Lund almost staggered with shock. "You—want to *help* me?"

"You're the best electronics supplier in the business," Antonio said. "It would be inconvenient for me if you went bust."

"How can I ever repay you," the man whispered, choking up, reaching out to shake his hand.

Antonio pulled away, pushing a card into his hand. "Don't thank me. Just contact my lawyers."

Lund shook his head in wonder. "Why, Delacruz? You've always been a shark. Why would you save me?"

"It's a business decision, nothing more," Antonio blurted out, and fled. Stepping out into the privacy of the hallway outside his ballroom, he called his lawyers. Afterward, as he returned to the crowded ballroom, with all its music and flowers, he still couldn't understand why he'd done it. He'd had an excellent chance of buying the shares cheap and taking control of the company at a stellar profit. What was wrong with him?

Hana. She was what was wrong. It wasn't

enough that she'd gained the loyalty of his employees and tried to take over his company. She was starting to make Antonio doubt his own priorities.

You've always been a shark.

His hands tightened. It wouldn't be enough to get Hana out of his company, he suddenly realized. He needed her out of his soul. Out of his heart.

Antonio felt the shiver of ice down his spine, the one he always felt when he felt the air around him changing. Gritting his teeth, he pushed the feeling aside. He just liked the American company's cockpit instrument displays, that was all. As Lund had said, the bigger airline would have consumed it whole. Their CEO was a corporate bloodsucker.

It had been a stone-cold business decision, nothing more. His priorities were strength and profit, like always. He hadn't changed. He was his own man. He made his own fate.

Hana would sign the post-nup tonight, and tomorrow he'd fly off to New York. For the foreseeable future, he would be so busy building his empire that their only connection would be in bed, or to discuss matters regarding their child's welfare. He'd give his wife free rein at home and she'd have no complaints.

Grabbing a glass of scotch, he drank it down in a single gulp and deposited the empty glass on a passing tray. He saw his wife speaking to some French aerospace executives he recognized. As he approached, he heard the executives eagerly telling Hana about their latest technology. She responded with sharp, incisive questions that made the other men laugh, with admiring glances. Coming from behind, Antonio kissed her softly on the temple.

Hana turned to look at him. "Where have you been?"

"Investing in avionics," he said lightly.

"We'd heard about your wife," one of the executives told him jovially, smiling at Hana. "But the rumors didn't do her justice. It's a pleasure, madame."

She grinned. "Just remember that when we discuss that discount for our next order."

"You drive a hard bargain."

She was obviously still representing herself as a leader in his company. Repressing his irritation, Antonio gave the executives a bland smile. "Will you excuse me, gentlemen? My wife and I are supposed to lead the first dance."

As he led Hana onto the dance floor of the *palacio*'s ballroom, a hush fell across the crowd. At his sign, music began to play from the orchestra. Pulling her into his arms, Antonio held her against his tuxedo-clad body, the two of them alone beneath a spotlight on the ballroom dance floor.

Her arms in long white gloves wrapped around the shoulders of his black jacket, as the skirts of her blue ball gown fluttered against his legs. Her baby bump pressed against his muscled belly as his hands went to the small of her back. He felt her sway. Her brown eyes glowed with warmth, and her diamond tiara and jeweled necklace sparkled with fire beneath the chandeliers high above.

Hana was so beautiful. His hands tightened on her back. In this moment, in spite of all his promises to himself to be his own man and make his own fate, all he could feel was her.

Right here, in his arms, Hana was everything he'd ever wanted.

I love you. Just three little words. Why were they so hard for her to say?

As Hana swayed in her husband's arms, beneath the ballroom spotlight, as she looked up into his dark, unfathomable gaze as the orchestra's music swelled around them, telling him she loved him wasn't just hard—it was impossible.

All too soon, other guests joined them on the dance floor, bumping up against them, watching them, smiling at them—and the moment was lost.

She had to tell him. It was her only way to change the course of their lives. She had to be brave enough to finally speak words she could never take back.

Either Antonio would realize he loved her as well, and they could be happy...or else he'd tell her he couldn't. And they wouldn't.

The stakes were so high, it terrified her.

She couldn't say the words.

Hours later, when the ball finally ended and the last guest departed in the wee hours of the morning, Antonio turned to her with a smile. "Are you pleased?"

"Pleased?" she repeated, searching his gaze.

"You did a good job, Hana." He tilted his head. "You raised a lot of money tonight for charity, and gained goodwill and good press for CrossWorld." He paused. "Perhaps you could continue running the kids' charity. From home."

"I suppose." It had been a long day. They'd already told the house staff to go to bed. Tomorrow would be soon enough to tidy up.

Hana felt weary as she looked at Antonio in the darkened ballroom. The sweet smell of wilting flowers wafted around them as candles flickered to an end. She asked in a low voice, "Why don't you want me in the company anymore?"

Antonio hesitated. "You know why."

"Why?"

"Because I want you to have the freedom to be home. Taking care of our baby."

"But there's more to it than that, I know there is—"

"Did you sign the post-nup?"

"Yes." Her heart was pounding. *I signed it because I love you.* Why couldn't she say it?

"Where is it?"

"I left it in the bedroom."

"So you agree to the terms?"

"Yes." She'd barely skimmed the contract, as she'd been in a hurry to get ready for the party. But she'd have physical custody of their child, which was all she cared about. The money didn't matter.

"Good." He gave a brief nod. "I hope you feel the financial settlement was generous."

"Yes. Thank you," she said numbly, because he seemed to be waiting for a response. Did he expect her to be grateful to him for carefully planning their divorce, when all she wanted was for him to love her?

She had to tell him.

Her body temperature suddenly went up twenty degrees. Feeling hot and afraid, she pulled off her long white gloves. Abruptly changing the subject, she said brightly, "I heard a rumor this evening."

"Rumor?" Antonio watched her peel the long gloves down her arms, one by one. A hunger came into his eyes.

"I can hardly believe it," she continued.

"Believe what?" His gaze fell onto her lips, his hard-edged face half in shadow. He looked devastatingly handsome in his perfectly cut tuxedo.

She smiled. "I heard a rumor that you not only let Horace Lund off the hook, you gave him a loan so his company would survive."

His dark eyes flashed up to hers, looking almost vulnerable, as if she'd caught him doing something wrong.

"So?" His tone was dismissive.

She didn't understand. "I'm glad."

His jaw hardened in the guttering candlelight.

"You need to stop trying to interfere with my company."

His company. For such a brief amount of time, it had been *their* company. The lump returned to her throat and she looked away. "You mean when I was discussing the new aircraft with Pierre."

"It's not your place."

Heart aching, Hana lifted her gaze to his and said, "I don't know where my place is anymore."

Taking her hands in his own, he lowered his head and kissed the back of each one.

"In my home," he whispered. "In my bed."

Their eyes met. Still holding her hand, he led her out of the shadowy ballroom and down the hall. He pulled her up the sweeping staircase, beneath the chandelier soaring high overhead, and the gaze of the angelic cherubs regarding them from the painted ceiling.

The *palacio* was strangely quiet, in the darkest hours of night, with all the servants long gone to bed. Their footsteps echoed against the tile as he led her down the hallway to their bedroom.

Closing the door behind him, he set her back gently on the bed, then fell to his knees on the priceless Turkish rug in front of her. Without a word, he untied each of her stiletto sandals, one by one, sending them skittering to the floor.

Rising to his feet, he slowly undid his cuff links and pulled off his black tuxedo jacket. His hard, handsome face was edged with moonlight from the window as he unbuttoned his shirt.

Her heart started to pound, in rhythm to the words she could not say. *I love you.*

His hard-muscled chest was lightly dusted with dark hair, his skin hot and smooth beneath the rough bristles as he lifted her back to her feet as if she weighed nothing. Unzipping the back of her blue Regency-style ball gown, he let it drop to the floor, leaving her standing in front of him in nothing but white lace panties, cut low to fit beneath her swelling belly, and a white lace demi-bra that barely contained her overflowing breasts.

Reaching around her, he undid the clasp, and her bra dropped to the floor as her breasts sprang free. With a flick of his fingers, he ripped the edges of the panties, and that white scrap of lace, too, fell to the floor.

"You don't have to destroy them—" she protested, then her mouth went dry when she saw the heat in his dark gaze.

Antonio cupped her face with his hands. "This

is just as I always pictured you," he whispered. "Naked, filled with my child." His fingertips lightly stroked the diamond and sapphire necklace above her bare collarbone. "Covered only with jewels."

She could not make herself say the words. *I love you.* But perhaps she could show him…

Hana pushed him back gently against the bed. Surprised, he looked up at her with smoldering eyes.

Leaning over, she kissed him. His sensual lips were warm and intoxicating. She wondered if he, too, was trying to tell her he loved her, because that was how he kissed her. Oh, if only it could be true…

Looking down at him, she pulled off the sparkling diamond tiara and set it on the nightstand. As if it were a striptease, she slowly pulled off all the hairpins from her ballerina bun, one at a time, tossing them to the floor.

Lying on the bed beneath her, he watched her, his eyes wide, his lips parted.

Looking down at him through her sweep of black eyelashes, she deliberately pulled the last hairpin from the bun. Shaking her head, she let her long dark hair tumble down her naked shoulders in the silvery moonlight.

Lowering her head, she kissed him, as the dark curtain of hair fell around her, brushing against his chest. Reaching up, he gripped her shoulders and kissed her, long and hard, his tongue plundering hers.

"Careful." Pulling back, she gave a low laugh, running the tip of one fingernail down his hard-muscled chest. "Remember I'm pregnant." She let the nail dig a little deeper. "You have to be very, very gentle with me..."

"I'm always gentle," he growled, his deep voice booming against the high ceiling of the nineteenth-century Spanish bedroom. Taking a deep breath, he repeated in a calmer voice, "I can be gentle." But even as his grip on her shoulders loosened, she saw the barely restrained wildness in his eyes.

As she kissed him, as she pulled off his tuxedo trousers and silk boxers beneath, she controlled the pace. If he tried to hold her, she stopped. If he tried to kiss her too passionately, she pulled away. She was tender. Gentle.

Finally, when she'd tortured him enough, she climbed over his naked hips and spread her bare legs wide over his thighs. She lowered herself on him, inch by inch, until beads of sweat appeared on his forehead from the effort of restraining his desire. She began to ride him. Slowly. Deliberately. Until he was gasping and gripping the comforter beneath him and nearly weeping as he held himself back. Tension coiled inside her, delicious and sweet, until she soared with a loud cry. A split second later, with a shout, he exploded inside her.

She'd been trying to show him that she loved him with her touch, since she was too terrified to tell him with words. But as they held each other afterward in bed, naked, sweaty and spent, as he kissed her tenderly on the forehead and said huskily, "You're incredible, *querida*, there's no other woman like you on earth," suddenly, Hana was no longer afraid.

"I need to tell you something," she whispered in the darkness. Wrapping his arms more securely around her, he pulled her back against his naked chest.

"What is it, *querida*?" he said drowsily, nuzzling her neck. His muscular body felt so warm against her own, making her feel safe. She took a deep breath.

"I love you, Antonio."

CHAPTER ELEVEN

ANTONIO'S EYES FLEW open in the dark bedroom.

I love you.

He'd been exhausted and content, holding his naked wife in his arms in the moonlight. But when he heard her whisper those three words with a mix of shyness and pride, he felt a rush of emotion.

I love you. Those soft, warm words poured like honey into all of his broken places.

I love you. Strange. Women had said those words to him before, but he'd always been cynical about it, assuming they were an obvious ploy meant to lure him into marriage.

This was different.

Hearing Hana say she loved him was like the first time he'd made love to her, when her innocence had almost made him feel as if he, too, were a virgin. Now, as he looked down at her in his arms, naked in their bed, he felt his heart swell all the way to his throat as he realized that he—

His shoulders stiffened as a cold sweat broke out along his spine.

No. Coldness rushed into his soul like wolves howling in a winter forest, biting the edges of his heart, making it shrink, making it bleed.

Antonio couldn't love her. He couldn't love anyone. If he ever really opened up, if he ever showed her all his flaws and darkness, her so-called love would evaporate like mist in the brutal Spanish sun.

Even his own parents hadn't wanted him. Neither had any of the foster parents who'd tried, or that waitress he'd naively tried to love at eighteen. They'd all seen some monstrous flaw in him. Why should he think that Hana, so intelligent and wise, wouldn't as well?

You'll never be good enough for her. You know it. I know it. And soon, Hana will know it, too.

Squeezing his eyes shut, he tried to push away Tanaka's words and return to that drowsy, contented feeling of a moment before. But it was impossible.

Hana was looking at him with her brown eyes full of tortured hope. She'd just told him she loved him. She was waiting for his answer.

But even if she believed she loved him now, it wouldn't last. Soon she would open her beautiful brown eyes and see that he was unworthy of her. She'd turn away. She'd scorn him.

She'd leave.

At the thought, ice spread across Antonio's body, from the tips of his fingers and toes toward his center, flash-freezing every cell and nerve, racing up his spine. Ice reached his heart, cracking into shards.

Hana sat up in bed, her lovely face worried. "Antonio?"

"I—" Was he having a heart attack? Was he dying? His breathing was hoarse. His heart felt like it had stopped beating. He had to control the situation. He couldn't let her realize the truth—

"What's wrong?" she said anxiously, putting her hand on his bare shoulder.

Jerking away, he nearly fell out of the bed. "Where is the post-nup?"

With bewildered eyes, she pointed to the end table by the fireplace. Stumbling over, he found the pages, saw her signature at the bottom. *Hana Delacruz.* The postnuptial agreement had been more generous than his lawyers had liked, but they'd mostly been relieved that one now existed. "You have to get her to sign this immediately, *señor.* Your whole life is at risk."

But Antonio didn't feel better now that he held the financial document in his hands. Because it wasn't just his business empire that was at stake.

He couldn't look at her, at those brown eyes that had started to lose hope. Grabbing clothes from the enormous walk-in closet, he pulled on jeans and a long-sleeved T-shirt. He grabbed a Louis Vuitton duffel bag.

"Where are you going?" Hana exclaimed.

He kept his voice expressionless. "New York."

"So early? Surely you don't have to leave in the middle of the night!"

"My competitors don't rest. Neither can I."

She seemed to shrink a little on the bed, pulling the blanket up higher, over her belly, all the way to her neck.

"How can you leave me like this?" she whispered. "I just told you I love you!"

Antonio didn't look at her as he roughly put clothes in the duffel bag. "I never asked for your love."

"I know." She took a deep breath. "When we married, I didn't want your love, either. I was afraid if we fell in love, our child might feel excluded, as I once did, from parents focused only on each other. But now I know it doesn't have to be that way. I can love you both. So much."

He paused. "You can love me if you want. But I'm not like you. I don't have…"

"Feelings?" she choked out.

"The ability to love you in such a sentimental fashion. I'll never be like Tanaka, mooning over you all the time. I care for you and our child. Caring is an action, not an emotion. I will always provide for you and the children. But CrossWorld Airways is what I love. It's the only thing I can control. The only thing that lasts."

"Family doesn't last? Love?"

He gave a low, bitter laugh. "No. Love doesn't last."

Hana's expression suddenly changed. "Why don't you admit the truth?"

"And what's that, Hana?"

"You're afraid to love me. Just as you're afraid to find out the truth about your parents. But the worst thing is, you *like* being afraid. Because it's safe." She lifted her chin. "You're a coward, Antonio."

His body recoiled.

Then cold anger snapped his spine straight, made his shoulders broaden to their full width. He looked at her, his soul like ice. "Enough."

He snapped the bag shut. "If you ever speak of love again, this marriage is over."

And without looking at her again, he left.

Hana woke to hear the shutters opening. Rich Spanish sunlight poured in from the wrought-iron veranda overlooking their grand tree-lined avenue in Madrid.

"*Buenos días*, Señora Delacruz," Manuelita chirped happily.

But it wasn't a good morning. With a sudden sick feeling, Hana remembered everything that had happened during the darkness, hours before.

Her husband didn't want her love.

So much so that when she'd told him she loved him, he'd literally packed his bag and left the country.

Hana's whole body hurt from a night of tossing and turning. Glancing at the gilded clock over the marble fireplace mantel, she saw it was nearly eleven. She must have fallen asleep shortly before dawn. Now, sunlight flooded their bedroom.

But it might as well have been pouring rain.

She sat up stiffly in the big four-poster bed, yanking the comforter up over her nightgown.

Her joints ached, and her lower back. Her hugely pregnant belly felt heavy. So did her heart.

Picking up a breakfast tray from a nearby table, Manuelita brought it to the bed. "Señor Delacruz told me yesterday that whenever he travels, we must take extra good care of you." She smiled. "He asked me to wake you up each morning with a tray, and your favorite flower."

Hana looked down at the tray in her lap. The breakfast had all her favorites—fruit, yogurt, crusty toast and jam, scrambled eggs, with orange juice and herbal tea. And in a tiny, perfect crystal vase, a tiny, perfect pink rose.

"Thank you, Manuelita," she whispered. Smiling, the older woman left with a satisfied nod, as if proud of representing her employer, who had obviously become a romantic, leaving his pregnant wife to sleep in and arranging breakfast in bed, even remembering her favorite flower. So romantic, so loving, so thoughtful.

But it didn't feel that way to Hana. Antonio had no problem paying people off with money or gifts. He'd asked his housekeeper to take care of Hana. But giving her anything real of himself—his time, his trust, his *love*—forget it.

Hana gulped water, dehydrated after her night

of tears. She tried to eat a few bites of food, but it all tasted like ash in her mouth.

Staring at the little flower, she resisted the urge to crumple it in her hand. Rather than trying to comfort her over the painful fact that he couldn't love her, or apologizing over the way he'd kicked her out of the company she'd come to love, Antonio had simply left. So she couldn't argue with him. She didn't even have a chance.

It was a coldhearted way to win. Ruthless. Exactly the way Antonio always dealt with his mistresses, opponents and rivals.

She'd just never thought he'd treat her like that. Pushing the breakfast tray aside, she walked across the cool tile floor with bare feet. She pulled on a red silk robe with an embroidered dragon on the back. Opening a side door, she peeked into the baby's empty nursery. She'd spent hours tenderly picking out the furniture, the crib, the glider, the books, the toys. A huge stuffed polar bear rested against the corner of the pale pink walls. She loved this room, where very soon they'd bring their baby home. Her husband had barely looked at it.

Just as he'd barely looked at Hana when he left.

Turning back to the master bedroom, she

opened the French doors. With a deep breath of the fresh, cool air, she went out onto the balcony, overlooking the historic neighborhood of Madrid where they lived.

Vivid pink bougainvillea hung on the edges of the wrought-iron balcony. Blinking fast, she looked out at the classical cream-colored buildings and palm trees beneath the golden sun and blue sky. A cold wind blew against her skin. Autumn had truly come at last. And along with it, the cold truth she hadn't wanted to face.

Her husband was broken, and her love could not save him. Because he did not even want to be saved.

Hana's hands tightened on the wrought-iron balcony. She had to find a way out of this. *Had* to. Why had he forced her to leave the company? They could easily set up a nursery in the office after the baby was born. Since she knew Antonio had no intention of spending less time at work, their only hope to be close as a family was for their family to be at work, as well. Surely he had to see this.

But he didn't want to see it. He was deliberately pushing her and the baby away.

Her cell phone rang from her bag inside. Turning back to the bedroom, she grabbed it, praying it was Antonio calling to make amends. But it wasn't her husband's name displayed on her phone, but someone even more surprising.

"Hello?" she said, a little nervously.

"Hana." Ren Tanaka's deep voice was tentative. "I almost didn't expect you to answer."

"Ren," she whispered, feeling low. "How did you know?"

"Know what? Is something wrong?"

She bit her lip. They hadn't spoken since her wedding day in Tokyo. She didn't know where to begin. "I…it's hard to explain."

"I'm sorry. I shouldn't have ignored you for the last six months," Ren said quietly. "I just… didn't know how to deal with everything."

"I know."

"I'm in Paris. I wondered if I could come see you." He paused. "I have some news."

Hana knew her husband wouldn't like her seeing Ren. He'd made his thoughts clear on her having a best friend who was a man: it wasn't allowed.

But it was so unfair. Antonio had abandoned her, cutting her off even from work. Did he expect her to remain a lonely prisoner in this house?

Forget that.

"Please come as soon as you can," she said, her voice cracking. "I need a friend today."

After they hung up, she paced all afternoon, staring at her phone, wishing Antonio would call her, trying to resist the urge to call him. He'd surely arrived in New York by now. She wondered how the negotiations were going with the labor union. Hana had always been the buffer.

Finally, she could resist no longer. Snatching up the phone, she dialed his number.

Antonio didn't answer. It rang and rang, then went to voice mail. She tried again. The same. She felt sick, questioning the future of their marriage. She was desperate to find something, anything, that would give her hope.

In the meantime, Antonio couldn't even be bothered to answer the phone.

She didn't leave a message. What was there to say?

When Ren showed up at the door of the *palacio* later that night, they hugged awkwardly over her enormous belly. Ren looked different, Hana thought. He'd grown a beard, and his clothes were more youthful.

Manuelita brought tea into the salon, then left, looking back between them suspiciously.

"Does she think I've come here to seduce you?" Ren said, his lips quirking.

Hana tried to smile, blinking so fast he wouldn't see the tears in her eyes. "Yes, a heavily pregnant woman is always a seduction magnet."

They sat on opposite couches in the salon for an hour drinking tea, making small talk about inconsequential things, people they knew, the expansion of the Tanakas' hotel business in Tokyo. Finally, with the pastries all gone and the tea grown cold, Ren looked at her across the coffee table.

"You look well, Hana," he said softly. "Are you happy?"

She set down her china teacup and changed the subject. "What's your big news?"

Leaning forward, Ren pulled a small black velvet box out of his pocket. Opening the lid, he held it out to her. A huge, sparkling diamond engagement ring.

Hana's mouth fell open with horror. "Oh, no—Ren, you know I'm already…and besides—"

"Hana, relax!" With a laugh, Ren snapped the lid closed. "It's not for you!"

"Whew!"

Staring at each other, they both burst into laughter, the awkwardness suddenly gone.

"You should see your face," he said, grinning.

"I'm sorry," she said. "But you scared me! For six months, you haven't answered my messages. I had no idea what you were feeling!"

"I know." His face grew serious. "The night you left Tokyo, you broke my heart."

Hana felt awful. "I never meant to."

"I know." He squared his shoulders. "I came to thank you. For telling me what I needed to hear."

"Even though I broke your heart?"

Ren shook his head. "It hurt, but not as much as my years of silent longing and hoping before. It's why I hated Delacruz from the moment you started working for him. I could hear the way you spoke about him." He paused. "But when you told me you'd never love me, as hard as it was to hear, it freed me. I was finally able to move on. And now... I'm happier than I've ever been."

"You've found someone else," she guessed.

He nodded shyly. "That's the other news I wanted to share. Emika Ito—you remember her?"

"The head of the Tokyo lead team?"

Ren nodded. "The night of your wedding, she

came over and started talking to me. She's a good person, a kind person."

"And pretty," Hana added slyly.

"Yeah. That, too." He grinned. "We ended up doing shots at the bar and then…"

"Then?"

Happiness glowed from him. "The next day, she wanted to check on me, just to see I was all right. And gradually, our friendship turned into more." Ren shook his head. "It's strange. When you left Tokyo, I thought my heart would be broken forever." He looked down at the ring. "I never imagined how wonderful it could be to have someone love me like Emika does. And the way I love her! It makes me realize… My love for you was never real." He gave her a crooked grin. "I hope you're not offended."

"I'm thrilled!"

"Yesterday, I was finishing a conference in Paris, and I decided I couldn't wait any longer. I went to a jeweler and bought this ring. I'm going to ask her to marry me as soon as I'm back in Tokyo. I'll throw a big party, do everything I can to show her how much I love her. And I thought…" He lifted his gaze. "Who else could I share this big news with, if not my best friend?"

Tears lifted to Hana's eyes. Ren was in love.

He was getting married. And in spite of all their past troubles, he'd come to share the news with her. "I'm so glad."

"Thank you." He tucked the black velvet box back in his pocket. Then his voice changed. "But what about you? Are you happy, Hana?"

"Of course," she said automatically, then flinched at the wobble in her voice.

Ren's jaw tightened. "Tell me what's wrong."

She gave him a sad smile. "You might be my best friend, but I can't tell you about my marriage."

"I understand."

"You do?"

He shrugged. "I've always thought Delacruz was a jerk. You know that. But if Emika and I were having a fight, I wouldn't want her to run tell some other man about it. I'd want her to talk to me, so we could work through it."

"Some things can't be worked through," Hana whispered.

His eyes narrowed. "He's hurt you—cheated on you?"

She was aghast. "No!"

"Then?"

"He…he just doesn't want to share his life

with me, not really. He doesn't want to share his heart."

"Maybe he's afraid." His eyes met hers. "I get it. But love can fix the broken pieces. I've learned that better than anyone. Maybe your heart won't be the same as it was, but—" the corners of his lips lifted "—it can be repaired, and more precious and beautiful for all that."

Her throat ached with pain. *"Kintsugi."*

Ren looked thoughtful. "Yes, I suppose you could look at it like that. A broken heart repaired by love."

Unable to speak, Hana looked out the large window of the *palacio*'s grand salon, overlooking the courtyard filled with orange trees. "But if Antonio doesn't love me…"

"There are all kinds of love." He snorted. "Maybe he has the kind of love that made him want to smash my face in back in Tokyo." He gave a sly grin. "Not that he would have succeeded, mind you…"

"He's possessive, yes. He keeps what is his." She strove to keep the bitterness out of her voice. "But that's not love."

Ren leaned over the coffee table. "Give him a chance, Hana. Tell him how you feel."

"I tried, and he…he just left."

"So try again."

Swallowing, she lifted her gaze. "But what if he really, truly can't love me?"

"Then at least you'll know." His eyes met hers. "Don't be like me, suffering for years in silence. Find out the truth. It's better to know, even if it hurts. It's the only thing that can set you free from a prison of hope."

A prison of hope. Hana shivered, looking down at her cooling tea. What a frightening thought. Even cold, awful freedom had to be better than that.

Ren looked regretfully at his watch. "I'm so sorry. I have to catch my flight to Tokyo." He rose to his feet. "You'll come to our wedding, won't you?" He gave a nervous laugh. "Assuming Emika says yes."

"Of course she'll say yes." Rising to her feet in turn, Hana walked him to the door. "And of course I'll come."

Pausing at the doorway, Ren said, "Give him another chance. Men can be fools." He added cheerfully, "And Delacruz is the biggest fool I've ever met."

"You two," she said, rolling her eyes.

He grinned. "We both love you. In different ways."

She returned his smile, then it faded. "He says he doesn't."

Ren sobered. "Maybe he doesn't. Or maybe he wants to, but he can't. Because of something he's gone through. Something he's lost," he said quietly. "Something he needs to get over, like I needed to get over you."

Hana thought of Antonio's childhood, the repeated abandonment when he was a boy. She said slowly, "What if he doesn't want to get over it?"

His eyes looked troubled. Then he shook his head. "Love can conquer anything. You'll see." He grinned. "Even that arrogant Spanish bastard."

After he was gone, Hana felt alone in the big, empty room. She paced, her angry footsteps echoing against the walls.

Love could conquer anything, could it?

But it hadn't! It couldn't!

Could it?

She stopped, clenching her hands at her sides as she looked out the big windows at the courtyard. She took a deep breath. After everything he'd gone through, it was no wonder Antonio wouldn't want to risk loving anyone, ever again.

If Hana could only find a way to heal him!

If he'd just been willing to learn why his parents abandoned him on those church steps the day he was born, she thought. Maybe the truth would hurt him—but like Ren had said, wouldn't knowing be better than always wondering? A wound couldn't heal until you removed the thing that was making it fester.

But Antonio had burned the letter. Closing her eyes, she tried to remember the doctor's name. Moreno? *Mendoza*. From some funny Basque-sounding village. Eche—something.

"Did your friend leave?" Manuelita called as Hana hurried back down the hallway.

"Yes." Going into the study, she grabbed her laptop and sat down at her husband's desk. Opening it, she started searching online. Hours later, after her shoulders ached with being hunched over the screen, she found it.

Dr. Mendoza. Of Etxetarri.

For a moment, she hesitated, knowing Antonio might never forgive her for intruding. But if her husband had no desire to heal his pain, no desire to love or be loved—no desire to even be in the same room with her!—how could they remain married? He'd told her if she ever mentioned love again, their marriage was over!

With a deep breath, Hana picked up her phone.

Her hands shook as she dialed the doctor's listed number, and listened to it ring.

And when it was finally answered, Hana learned—everything.

CHAPTER TWELVE

WHEN ANTONIO GOT the first phone message from his wife, he ignored it.

And the second, third and fourth.

For the last three days, he'd been struggling in the boardroom of CrossWorld's New York office, dealing with his team of lawyers. Lauren, his new executive assistant in the New York office, hadn't done the prep work as thoroughly as Hana would have. Nor did she have the same charm.

But no one was as good as Hana. On top of all his wife's skills with language, logistics and the airline business in general, she'd also worked side by side with Antonio for years, and knew how to manage him almost as well as she could manage the labor union.

The negotiations hadn't gone at all well without her. Antonio had been off his game. He didn't know why. Maybe because he hadn't slept well alone in the luxury New York hotel suite. The bed felt empty.

So when he saw, on the third day as he'd come out of yet another fruitless, combative meeting, that Hana had left him yet another message, he'd just gritted his teeth and ignored it. He didn't need her at his company. He could do very well without her.

Especially if she was calling to gloat over his failure.

He glanced at his watch. He was late for a 9:00 p.m. dinner with Horace Lund. He'd think of Hana later.

I love you. He heard her voice. Remembered the pain in her eyes when he hadn't responded as she'd hoped he might.

No. Antonio couldn't bend. If he did, he was afraid he'd break.

Over appetizers in the elegant midtown restaurant, after Horace Lund toasted his gratitude for Antonio's loan, the older man spoke cheerfully about his business's potential. But by the man's third bourbon, he became morose. As he ate his fettuccine, he spoke about his recent divorce. By dessert, he was nearly crying over his cannoli.

"My wife always complained I didn't spend enough time with her," the older man choked out. "So last week, she said I should be happy she was divorcing me, because now I can work every single minute without guilt, just as I wanted..." And on and on.

Antonio, who'd indulged in only one glass of scotch, tried not to roll his eyes as he sipped bitter black coffee for dessert. He despised the man's tearful regret. If Lund didn't want this to happen, he never should have let himself love his wife. Why else was Antonio avoiding Hana? Even in spite of the unfortunate impact on his company.

The negotiations had gone badly again today, and the head of the employees' union had asked point-blank for Hana. "She, at least, knows what the employees are up against." Antonio had responded coldly, "You're up against *me*." And before he knew what was happening, the other man was stomping out of the meeting. Antonio ground his teeth.

"Now she's fallen for some yoga instructor," Lund moaned, as he stuffed cannoli into his mouth. "He doesn't have a penny but she doesn't care..."

Antonio regretted yet again that he'd ever agreed to meet the man for dinner. He coughed, then said tersely, "Pull yourself together. She's gone. It's time to move on. You have a company to reorganize."

"Yes." Lund brightened, then his lip began to wobble again. "Patricia helped me start it. It's not the same without her..."

Antonio was contemplating the possibility of flinging himself out the Italian restaurant's large glass window to get away from the man's whining when he heard his phone ping. Relieved for the distraction, he glanced at it. A message from Hana flashed across the screen.

I spoke with your mother. I know everything. You should come home.

Antonio jumped to his feet. His whole body was suddenly shaking. "I have to go," he said hoarsely, and tossed money on the table before he fled beneath the man's astonished eyes.

Getting into his Rolls-Royce waiting outside, Antonio was on the phone before his driver even pulled from the curb, contacting his new secretary. "Cancel tomorrow's meetings with the union."

"What?" Lauren's young voice was shocked. "Are you—are you sure, sir?"

He knew the question she'd nearly blurted

out was, *Are you crazy?* A man messed with
the union at his peril. But everything that had
seemed so important suddenly meant nothing,
compared to the acid hissing through his soul,
searing everything in its path. "Have the jet
waiting for me at Teterboro."

By the time his plane touched down in gray,
rainy Madrid, it was early afternoon. Far from
sleeping on the flight, he'd paced the aisle of
his Gulfstream jet, his body so tight, his muscles hurt. As his driver took him to the *palacio*,
through the city's crowded, lively streets in the
autumn drizzle, Antonio looked out the window
with a churning feeling in his belly.

What had Hana learned? The horrible thing
that had made him a monster from the day he
was born?

I spoke with your mother. I know everything.

The driver passed the *palacio*'s gatehouse and
pulled into the courtyard. Antonio was already
opening his door before the car stopped. Jump-
ing out, he rushed inside, his heart pounding.

Empty. The *palacio* was empty.

Ice gripped his heart as he walked past dark
rooms filled with antiques, past the salon on the

main floor, with its big windows. Turning on a light, he went slowly up the sweeping staircase, feeling like he'd aged fifty years. He already knew what he would find: an empty bedroom, with all her clothes gone from their closet. All his attempts to hide his unworthiness from her had failed…

A light clicked on. He saw Hana sitting in the bedroom's armchair by the empty fireplace. There were dark circles beneath her eyes, as if she hadn't slept well in days, either.

Seeing her, Antonio felt a rush of joy. Then he was overwhelmed by fury. By betrayal.

"How could you?" Dropping his briefcase to the bedroom's tile floor, he ground out, "I made it clear I have no desire to learn about my past. Ever."

Hana lifted her chin, her eyes defiant. "I had to."

"Why? Do you hate me so much?"

She stopped, blinked. "No. I love you. That's why I did this. I'm trying to help you." Her expression became tender as she said softly, "You need to know the truth."

"But I burned that man's letter—"

"I remembered his name. I looked him up on

the internet and called him." She paused. "Yesterday, I took the train up to Etxetarri."

"Where?"

"A little fishing village to the north." She took a deep breath. "I met your mother. In person."

"You. What?" Sudden vertigo made him lightheaded.

"Please, just listen. You have to know. It could change everything. As Ren told me when he came here, the truth can set you free—"

Ren Tanaka? That made Antonio stop cold. All his fear and pain and uncertainty coagulated around this one point. "He was here?"

"You're missing the point—"

"You invited Tanaka to this house?" His eyes narrowed. "Behind my back? While I wasn't here?"

"*Behind your back?* Are you serious?" A hard laugh burst from her lips. "The only reason you weren't here is because *you left me*. In the middle of the night. After I told you I loved you."

Antonio thought of Lund's wife and the yoga instructor. "I told you I didn't want you to be friends with Tanaka anymore."

"Yes, you've told me a lot of things." She lifted her steady gaze to his. "Like when you said the company would belong to us equally. When you said we'd share our lives. But from the moment we arrived in Madrid, you've been pushing me away. And when I told you I loved you, you left."

She saw right through him. His weaknesses. He said coldly, "You keep bringing that up. But one has nothing to do with the other. And don't change the subject from Tanaka—"

"Ren came to show me the engagement ring he bought in Paris." For a split second, ice gripped Antonio's throat, before she continued, "He's going to propose to his girlfriend. Emika."

He stared at Hana blankly. "Emika?"

"Emika Ito," she prompted. "The head of your Tokyo office. Remember?"

"Of course I remember," he snapped. He took a deep breath, forcing his shoulders to relax. So Tanaka wasn't a rival after all. He felt dizzy with relief. "He came all the way to Madrid to tell you that?"

"Ren came to thank me. He told me it hurt him in April when I told him I'd never love him, but it also set him free," she said quietly. "When he was forced to give up old dreams, he was able to have new ones."

Her voice was strange. He set his jaw. "What are you trying to say?"

Hana's eyes met his. "You're afraid to let me love you. Because you're afraid to love me."

Antonio felt a wrench in his belly, a wild pounding of his heart even worse than when he'd heard about Tanaka's visit. *She knew.* This rocked the walls around his heart, the radioactive place he'd spent a lifetime being careful not to go. "Don't be ridiculous."

"But you don't have to be afraid. Not anymore." Rising to her feet, Hana came closer. Her eyes gleamed, her curvy pregnant body swaying as she approached. "I know the reason you were left on those church steps the day you were born."

"Stop," he said helplessly.

"Your mother's name is Josune Loiola. Here is her address. Her phone number." Hana held out a piece of paper. "Please go talk to her."

"No!" Ignoring the paper, he shook his head violently. "I don't want to know!"

"You have to hurry. There's not much time left. Your mother's sick. Dying…"

"I don't care."

"Only because you don't know what happened!"

"I know enough."

"You have to forgive her. So you can forgive yourself."

"Me?" Antonio looked at her incredulously. "I've done nothing wrong."

"Exactly. But you still can't move past it. And you must." Putting her hand on her pregnant belly, she murmured, "We need you."

"And this is how you try to help me?" Antonio said wildly. "By going behind my back, betraying me?"

"It's not a betrayal." When he still didn't move, she set the paper gently down on the side table. Coming forward, she put her hand on his arm. He imagined he saw pity in her eyes. "If you won't go see her, just listen. I'll tell you…"

Antonio yanked his arm away. "Stop it. Now. Or…"

"Or what?" As Hana stood apart from him, her lovely face suddenly looked sad. "Or you'll leave me again?"

"Yes."

He saw the exact moment hope died in her eyes.

Hana took a deep breath. "Don't bother."

Turning toward the door, she picked up a small overnight bag, the one she'd brought from Tokyo six months before. He frowned. "Where are you going?"

"To Tokyo," Hana said. "Ren's proposing to

Emika at a big party tomorrow. If I leave right now, I can be there." She looked back at him. "With friends who actually want me to be part of their lives." She looked around the master bedroom where they'd spent so many passionate nights. "I thought this could be my home. But home isn't a place. It's people who love you."

Antonio stared at her. Outside the wrought-iron balcony, the lowering gray clouds rattled the lead windows with rain.

The bedroom seemed to whirl in front of his eyes as he looked at his wife holding the bag. Fear twisted through him. Anguish. Anger. He clung to the last emotion, the only one he knew how to deal with.

"You can't leave," he ground out. "You're my wife. Carrying my child."

"And yet you made it clear if I ever spoke about love again, our marriage was over."

Antonio narrowed his eyes. "Is this because I changed my mind about giving you half my company?"

"It hurt when you went back on your promise." She gave him a wistful smile. "Sharing the company was like sharing you."

Antonio's heart hammered against his ribs.

"But I was dreaming." Hana turned away.

"I'm going to have my baby in Tokyo. I already booked myself on the evening flight. That, at least, is part of the post-nup I remember." She gave a smile. "Unlimited flights on CrossWorld Airways for the rest of my life."

"You knew this was how tonight would end," he said slowly.

"I've tried everything I can to help heal you. But if you don't want to be healed, there's nothing I can do. Loving you isn't enough. I can't love you if you won't love yourself."

He stared at her, feeling numb.

She took a deep breath, trying to smile. "Our baby will have your name when she's born. You can see her anytime you want, no matter what the post-nup says."

"Hana," he choked out.

Her beautiful eyes were luminous in the shadows of their bedroom, as if her heart was breaking. "Goodbye, Antonio."

She left without looking back.

There was a flash of lightning outside the bedroom's windows. Antonio felt numb. As thunder rumbled across the sky a moment later, he felt a gut-wrenching pain.

How could Hana leave him? She had no right. He would not allow it. *She was his.*

And yet…he felt a strange trickle down his spine. His body was reacting strangely. Beneath the anger, he felt pain, yes. But also, buried in the cracks, another feeling he couldn't understand. One that made no sense. Relief.

Finally.

He'd always known this would happen. Even in their happiest moments. Even when he'd been making love to her on a pink sand Caribbean beach on their honeymoon, part of him had always known he'd lose her. No, even before that. On their wedding day in Tokyo, when Ren Tanaka had told him he wasn't worthy of his bride. *And someday soon, Hana will know it, too.*

That day had finally come.

His eyes fell on the end table. All he could see, all he could feel, was the small paper that Hana had left there. His mother's address. Her phone number. The answers to everything he'd feared most.

Turning, he fled the room.

Antonio went downstairs to his study to try to work, but he couldn't concentrate on his laptop. Words and figures swam incomprehensibly in front of his eyes. He thought of how he'd judged Horace Lund so harshly at the restaurant in New York, and wondered if he himself would soon be muttering wild-eyed over cannoli about the woman he'd lost.

He hadn't lost Hana to a yoga instructor. Not even to Tanaka, who though he still hated him, Antonio grudgingly had to admit he had a certain unwilling respect for.

No. Antonio had lost her on his own. Because of his fear to learn the truth about his own darkest flaws.

Pushing his laptop aside in disgust, he left the study and went down the hall, nearly walking into an antique suit of armor. That was what Hana deserved, he thought. A knight in shining armor. A man who wasn't so deeply cracked at the core.

Going back to his bedroom, he yanked off the business suit he'd worn flying across the Atlantic, back when he'd thought he could still save their marriage. He put on exercise shorts, gym shoes and a thin T-shirt that stretched across his hard-muscled chest, then went back downstairs, past the kitchen, where he could hear Manuelita talking to her assistant and pounding the dough for bread. Going down the hall to his home gym, he turned on the light.

The gym was empty, gleaming, pristine. He pushed a button that lifted the automated blinds, filling the room with weak gray light.

I know the reason you were left on those church steps the day you were born.

Guzzling down some water from the cooler, he climbed on the treadmill. He set the speed faster and faster, trying to outrun his thoughts.

There's not much time left. Your mother's sick. Dying...

Going to the punching bag, he hit it without gloves. Once. Twice. He pounded it until his knuckles were raw.

I've tried everything I can to help heal you. But if you don't want to be healed, there's nothing I can do.

Antonio fell against the punching bag, wrapping his arms around it as his knees swayed beneath him.

Loving you isn't enough. I can't love you if you won't love yourself.

"Stop," he whispered aloud.

He didn't need her love. He had his business empire. His airline that allowed him to escape anywhere, anytime. He was a citizen of the world, beholden to no one and attached to nothing. He could replace Hana instantly. He…

Closing his eyes, Antonio leaned his hot cheek against the cool leather punching bag. He suddenly didn't care about his empire.

Money—what did that matter without being able to spend it on her?

Power—what kind of power could he ever have, if he didn't even have the power to be with her?

Sex—what appeal could meaningless hookups ever have, after the ecstasy of holding Hana in his arms?

His wife had tried to heal him. Ridiculous. Even she, with all her warmth and care, didn't have that power. He still couldn't believe Hana had tracked down the doctor and gone to speak with his mother.

There's not much time left. Your mother's sick. Dying…

A shudder went through him and he opened his eyes bleakly.

For the first time since he was a boy, he tried to picture his mother. Tried to imagine why she'd abandoned him. Was Antonio so awful as a newborn? Had he been colicky, crying for

hours? Had she hated the man who'd impreg-
nated her?

Had he been conceived, not in love, but out of
some horrific act like rape?

It was his greatest fear.

Antonio thought of his childhood, of not even
knowing who he was or why he'd been abandoned, of being sent back to the orphanage
whenever he'd dared hope he'd found someone
to love him, of getting beaten by the older kids
for crying. He'd simply learned to stop feeling
anything at all, just to avoid pain. He thought
of the time he'd imagined himself in love with
Isabella, giving his heart away so eagerly, only
to have it thrown back in his face. *Money is
what matters. Money is what lasts. You're young.
You'll learn.*

But Hana hadn't cared about money. She'd
only cared about him. Helping him. Healing
him.

Loving him.

Antonio shuffled wearily out of the home
gym. He stopped outside the doorway of the
grand salon, a gracious, high-ceilinged room,
in this palace once owned by a nobleman. The
decor was elegant, with all the prestige money
could buy. He'd done this to prove to everyone

that he was no longer the pathetic orphan he'd been. But there was one person he'd never been able to convince: himself.

I can't love you if you won't love yourself.

Suddenly, Antonio knew he had to make a choice. One choice now that would separate his life forever onto two different paths.

Which would it be?

Gripping his hands at his sides, he looked out the wide windows toward the orange trees in the rainy courtyard. Would he keep the life he'd had? Where he felt nothing, and controlled everything—most of all, his own feelings—out of fear?

Or would he take a risk?

Suddenly, he was tired of being afraid.

He'd lost Hana. What could be worse than that? What more did he have to fear?

Antonio stood totally still. Then his chin lifted, his jaw set.

He would no longer be enslaved by his worst fears about his past. About himself.

His spine snapped straight, and he turned on his heel. Going up the staircase, he went into his bedroom. He picked up the piece of paper Hana had left. He saw his mother's name, Josune Loiola. An address. A phone number.

Grabbing his phone, he started to dial, then stopped. No. He couldn't do this on the phone. He had to see the woman in person, to see her face, to demand why she'd left him as a baby, helpless and alone, in a basket on those church steps.

He dialed Garcia instead. "Gas up the jet."

"Back to New York, *señor*?"

"No," he told his bodyguard. "North. Tell the pilot to find the closest airport to a village called Etxetarri."

It was early evening when Antonio got into the car that awaited him on the tarmac of the tiny private airport on the northern coast. Getting into the car, he left Garcia and his pilot behind.

He had to do this alone.

Antonio's hands tightened on the wheel as he drove along the coastal road, following the directions of his GPS. The rain was thick here, and as the sun starting to lower toward the western horizon, a mist rolled in from the glassy gray sea.

Antonio felt butterflies in his stomach as he drove into the tiny fishing village with houses clinging to cliffs. Finally, he reached his destination, a squat stone building overlooking a bay filled with battered boats. And he blinked.

It was a hospice.

Its colorful shutters were bright against the gray stone and a profusion of flowers hung beneath the windows. Nervously, he parked his anonymous sedan behind the hospice and went inside. His clothes were anonymous as well, just a black T-shirt and dark pants. He didn't want this woman—this *stranger*—to imagine that he was trying to impress her. But his knees were shaking as he went inside.

"Who are you here to see?" the receptionist said, not looking up from her magazine.

"Señora Loiola."

"Her third visitor in two days," the girl murmured in surprise. "So many visits!" She looked up. "Are you expected, *señor*…?"

"Delacruz." Antonio saw the exact moment the receptionist recognized him. All those years he'd spent as the playboy billionaire of Madrid had apparently reached even this far north. "And no. She's not expecting me. We've never met."

"You're a friend?"

"Apparently—" he gave a hard smile "—I'm her son."

The young woman's jaw dropped. She rose hastily to her feet. "I'll show you to her room, Señor Delacruz."

Going down a short hallway, which was lit too brightly and smelled of antiseptic, she knocked on a door and peeked in. "Are you available for visitors, *señora*?" He couldn't hear the softly murmured reply. "There's a gentleman here who says he's your son."

The receptionist turned to him with a big, artificial smile. "Please. Go in."

Antonio hesitated, then squaring his shoulders, he turned to the door. From the corner of his eye he saw the receptionist surreptitiously taking his photo with her phone.

Inside, the room was dark, and filled with shadows. It took a moment for his vision to adjust.

Then he saw a small pitiful figure in the bed.

The woman was younger than he'd expected, perhaps in her midfifties, dark-haired and slender, with big dark eyes that seemed too large in her sunken, gaunt face. Especially now, when those eyes were glowing with almost painful hope.

"Is it really you?" she whispered. She took a shuddering breath. "My sweet boy?"

Antonio looked down at those dark eyes, so much like his own. And all of the air in his chest went out with a *whoosh*.

He'd come here to confront her, to accuse her of abandoning him as a baby, to berate her for what she'd done.

But he'd never once considered what might have happened to her.

He came forward into the shadowy room. On the table beside her, he saw a vase of fresh, vibrant flowers. Hana, he thought. It would be so like her to bring flowers to someone who was dying. Even a stranger.

"I'm Antonio," he said slowly. His voice cracked a little. "Delacruz is the last name the nuns gave me, when I was left on the steps of a church in Andalusia." He couldn't keep the recrimination from his voice.

The woman blinked fast. "I'm Josune," she whispered. "And I only learned yesterday that my baby lived. The baby I had thirty-six years ago." Tears were welling in her dark eyes. Her voice was almost too quiet to hear. She took a shuddering breath. "I was sixteen when you were born, and they told me you were dead. They told me—"

Her voice cut off.

He looked down at her.

His voice was strangely uncertain. "You...you didn't abandon me?"

"*Abandon* you!" Her black eyes blazed in her fragile face. "I never abandoned you, never!" She clasped her hands over the blanket in her lap. "Dr. Mendoza, my father, they both told me you died at birth. They wouldn't let me see your body. They said it would give me nightmares." She looked away sharply. Tears streaked down her face as she whispered, "If I'd known you were alive, if I'd ever even guessed…"

Antonio felt a razor blade in his throat. His voice was low and harsh. "Why would they tell you I was dead?"

She faltered, licking her cracked lips. "Your father was a backpacker from America. He'd come here to walk the Camino." She bit her lip. "I was very sheltered, and…"

Antonio could not breathe, looking down at her. His voice was a croak as he spoke his darkest fear. "He forced himself on you."

"Forced?" She snorted. "He romanced me. I wanted it to be love, but within the week, he was gone. He'd told me his name was John Smith. John Smith! Even my father could not find him, though he tried."

Antonio found himself sitting on the edge of her bed. "What happened?"

"My parents were ashamed their only daughter was pregnant and unwed. For a woman to have a child alone is ordinary now. Back then, it was not." She sighed. "Especially in a small village."

He glanced out the window, at the tiny stone village clinging to the cliffs above the sea. "But you still stayed here all your life."

"I'd shamed my family. Lost my baby. What else was I to do? My mother was sick. She needed me. She died a few years later, my father last year."

"But you could have married—had other children—"

Josune shook her head, her eyes full of tears. "I loved a man once, and he abandoned me. I had a child I loved. I lost him, as well." She looked away, toward the wild sea. "I couldn't ever face that pain again. Especially when I knew it was my fault."

"Your fault?"

Tears streamed down her sunken cheeks as she choked out, "When you died, the day you were born, what else could it be but my fault? I did something wrong. I wasn't good enough to be your mother." Looking away, she whispered, "I wasn't worthy of that kind of joy."

I wasn't worthy of that kind of joy.

Emotion gripped Antonio's heart. He thought of how he'd pushed Hana away. How he'd felt unworthy of her. How he'd tried not to love her, because he'd known he would only lose her.

"But yesterday your wife came to me," Josune said, her hand trembling as she reached toward the fresh flowers. "I could hardly believe it when she told me you were alive. I called Dr. Mendoza in a panic. He came to see me and confessed everything. My baby boy had been born healthy, but my father convinced him it would be better if they said you were dead. He took you to Andalusia, where no one in my village would hear of the baby who'd been found there." Her dark eyes lifted to his. "Yesterday I didn't know what to think, feel. It was as if all my dreams had come true—and my nightmares."

He could see the desperate question in her gaunt face. He said slowly, "Dr. Mendoza came to see me in Madrid recently. Why didn't he tell you about me then?"

"He said he didn't want to hurt me." Her lips turned up bitterly. "He was afraid, if you refused to see me, that it would only stir up new pain as I was already dying." She looked down at her slender hands, held together tightly on the blanket. "Even your wife wouldn't tell me her last name. She said the choice had to be yours." Lifting her gaze to his, she breathed, "I didn't think you would come, even as I prayed for it every moment. When I learned you were alive, I knew you must hate me..."

It was true, Antonio realized. He'd hated her every day. And hated himself for whatever had made them give him away.

"Just tell me you were happy," she begged. "Tell me you were adopted by a family who loved you, as I would have loved you every day. I would have called you Julen." Her gaze wandered to the window, overlooking the misty coast. "Waking up, I'd think, today my son would have been three. Today he would have been six. Today he would be eighteen, and a man." She looked back at him, and her dark eyes shone with tears like rain. "When I learned yesterday you were alive, it was almost too amazing to believe. But now, all I can think is that I should have known. I should have sensed you were alive, and come for you." Her voice broke as she said, "Please just tell me you were happy."

Antonio closed his eyes.

When he was young, he'd imagined what he would tell the parents who'd abandoned him, if he ever had the chance. How he'd destroy them with guilt. And he saw, in this moment, how easy it would be to destroy Josune. All the pain and anguish of his childhood was pounding in his memory as he opened his eyes and took a deep breath, knowing he could take his revenge just by telling her the truth.

"I was happy," he lied in a low voice. "I was loved."

She exhaled in a rush of tears, covering her face with her hands as she choked out a sob. "Thank you." She wiped her eyes. "But your wife is not with you today? You are expecting a baby. You said you live in Madrid?"

Antonio stared at her. She had no idea who he was, he realized. She wasn't asking about his fortune, or his airline. She wasn't looking at his net worth to determine his value. She was asking about what really mattered. His family.

And in a flash, things clicked into place.

Antonio had always thought he was different. That he, alone on earth, was unworthy of being loved. It had driven him to build a worldwide company, a billion-dollar fortune, to prove everyone wrong. To escape his worst belief about himself.

But the truth was, far from being a monster, he was exactly like everyone else. Flawed. Making the best decisions he could, and sometimes failing. Sometimes being wrong. So wrong.

But all along, he'd been loved, though he hadn't known it, every single day by his mother, who'd mourned him. And he'd been loved by Hana, even as he'd tried so hard to push her away.

"Can you ever forgive me, *mi hijo*?" Josune whispered.

Reaching out, he took his mother's trembling hands in his own. "There's nothing to forgive, *mama*."

With a cry, she reached her arms around her much taller, broad-shouldered son. He leaned forward to hug her, and for a moment, they held each other. Then finally, he pulled back.

"I love you, Antonio," his mother said, wiping the tears still glimmering in her eyes. "And your wife. For bringing you back to me."

He lifted his head. "My wife…"

Josune gripped his hand. "Never forget to tell her you love her. We always must tell each other. Because you never know how many chances we have."

Antonio looked at his mother as a crack of brilliant, warm gold light finally broke through the gray clouds.

Memory stirred. Gold through the cracks. He heard his wife's voice, telling him about broken Japanese pottery rejoined by solid gold. *Something broken and repaired is more precious and beautiful than something unused and whole. It shows history. It shows life.*

"You're right." Rising to his feet, Antonio said, "I'll be back as soon as I can."

"Go, my son."

Turning, he started running down the hall of the hospice, out into the misty village above the sea. To find his wife.

To find his heart.

CHAPTER THIRTEEN

"YES, OF COURSE I will marry you!"

Hana smiled as she watched her best friend rise eagerly to his feet and embrace the woman he loved. He'd proposed on one knee, holding out the diamond ring he'd shown Hana in Madrid, at a party he'd organized in a fantastic bar near Shibuya Square, surrounded by their family and friends.

Of course Emika had said yes, Hana thought, watching as the Japanese girl hugged Ren, her pretty face crying with happiness. Ren was beaming, looking like the proudest man in the world.

Hana watched them with a lump in her throat.

It was strange to be back in Tokyo, at another party in another hotel, celebrating another union of two people. But this was very different from the last.

Her own sort-of wedding reception had been more of a business celebration, actually, and held at a sleek, sophisticated luxury hotel. Then, it had been April, with the cherry trees brilliantly in bloom.

Ren and Emika's party was different. This bar was modern and colorful and hip, with brightly colored manga on the walls. It was on the second floor, with huge windows overlooking Shibuya Crossing, with all its big neon signs lighting up the night. It was the busiest pedestrian intersection in the world, where two thousand people or more could cross the street each time the light changed.

And yet, even surrounded by people, Hana felt alone.

She'd thought her love could save Antonio. She'd hoped, when she left him, he might come after her.

He hadn't.

Since their wedding, spring had turned to autumn. All the bright, innocent hope she'd felt the last time she'd been in Tokyo had been lost. Just like the cherry trees—her happiness had bloomed briefly, then faded, then fallen.

It was October now, the haunted, wistful month of longings and regret. Her baby was due in less than two weeks, and her whole body ached. She put her hands on her belly, which had been tensing up strangely all evening. Braxton Hicks contractions, she thought. And her lower back had been aching for hours, but what did she expect, after such a long flight? But just in case, she'd go to the doctor first thing in the morning.

"Are you feeling all right, Hana?"

Looking up, she saw Ren's worried face.

"Of course." Trying to smile, she nodded toward Emika, who was showing her diamond engagement ring to her clamoring, excited friends. "I'm so happy I got to see your proposal."

"I'm just happy she said yes," he replied wryly.

Hana smiled. "She loves you. Anyone can see that."

He came closer. He had a strange expression on his face. "Delacruz loves you. I know he does. Give him another chance…"

"More chances?" She felt pain in her heart just at hearing her husband's name. "I never thought you'd be the one to sing his praises."

"Me either." He bit his lip hard, then said only, "Just wait another hour. Have another melon soda. I promise you'll feel better in an hour."

Another hour of watching other people's happiness and feeling the pain of her own broken heart? She didn't think she could manage it. She evaded, "I'm going to go congratulate Emika."

As the next half hour passed, Hana listened to the engagement toasts, looking at the dreamy, dazzled faces of the happy couple, kissing each other and toasting a blissful future. Finally, she could bear it no longer. Taking her coat from the coatrack near the door, without saying farewell to anyone, Hana quietly left.

Outside, the Tokyo air was cold, with the bite of frost already looming in the air. The sidewalks were crowded, as it was Saturday night. The neon lights of Shibuya Crossing were bright, casting moving colors against the streets below, with all the noodle shops and tiny boutiques. Pulling her coat closer over her belly, she ducked her head and walked with the crowd toward her hotel, on the other side of the crossing.

Did she hear someone calling her name?

She shrugged it off. Hana was a common enough name in Japan. All her friends were still upstairs at the party.

Shivering, Hana waited on the sidewalk for the light to turn. When it did, all the cars stopped in the streets surrounding Shibuya Crossing, to wait for pedestrians. She moved with the crowds of people walking in every direction, even diagonally, across the large square.

Again, she thought she heard a voice shouting

her name. Grief must be making her crazy, because it sounded like Antonio. But her husband was back in Spain. Or perhaps he was already back in New York, negotiating with the employees' union. Because that was all he cared about: his empire. Not his wife. Not his child...

"Hana!"

This time, she couldn't stop herself from looking back.

And then she *knew* she was dreaming. Because there, in the middle of the street, she saw Antonio pushing toward her, his handsome face full of longing.

She stumbled in shock. It was only when he was suddenly there to catch her, and she felt the warmth and power of his arms, that she knew he was real.

"You're...you're here," she breathed.

"You left the party early..."

As he held her, she felt the current and flow of crowds passing all around them, but it was as if they were the only two people on earth as he lifted her gently back to her feet. Her forehead furrowed. "What are you doing here?"

His dark eyes burned through her. "I came for you."

"Why?"

"To tell you I was wrong. About everything." Antonio glanced around them as crowds continued to push past. "I saw my mother."

"What?"

Antonio gave a single nod. "I finally know the truth. About her. About myself. I've flown across the world to tell you what I've felt for a long time but was too scared to admit."

Her lips parted.

"You were right," he said simply. "I was a coward. You're the most incredible woman I've ever known. I was afraid I didn't deserve your love. And maybe I don't. But I can spend the rest of my life trying. Because you're my empire, Hana." Running his hands through her hair, he whispered, "You're my soul."

Glancing around them, she saw crowds thinning out. The crosswalk light was flashing green, indicating it was about to turn red, when the car traffic would return. "We should get off the street…"

"Tell me it's not too late," Antonio urged. "Tell me I still have a chance."

Looking up at him, she gave a low laugh. "Even Ren told me I had to give you another chance."

"I know. When I phoned him from the plane…"

Her jaw dropped. "You phoned Ren?"

"He wasn't glad to hear from me," Antonio said, rubbing his chin ruefully. "It took a lot of begging to convince him I deserved to see you again. He was supposed to keep you at the party till I arrived."

No wonder Ren had told her to drink another melon soda, and promised she'd feel better in an hour. An incredulous laugh bubbled from her as she shook her head. "You—begging Ren? That must have hurt."

Antonio snorted. "You have no idea." His grin faded. "But not nearly as badly as it hurt to think of losing you." His dark eyes seared hers. "I love you, Hana."

Her heart was pounding. They were still standing in the middle of the crossing. They had to move. She knew they had to move. But she couldn't. If this was a dream, she didn't want to wake.

They heard loud honks from the approaching cars.

"Hey, that's my pregnant wife you're honking at!" Antonio yelled at the cars, who really did have the right of way. Taking her hand, he gently pulled her to the sidewalk on the other side.

His hand tightened on hers as he faced her on

the crowded sidewalk. His gaze searched hers beneath the moving lights of the electronic billboards. "I love you," he repeated. He leaned his forehead against hers as he murmured, "Am I too late?"

Shaking her head, Hana drew back, smiling. "It's never too late." Lifting her hand, she placed it on his scratchy cheek. "Because I'll never stop loving you."

She heard his intake of breath. Pulling her into his arms, Antonio lowered his head to hers. His kiss was passionate, gentle and hot at once, promising forever.

Then Hana felt it again. The strange, sharp pain around her abdomen. Just like she'd read about. This wasn't Braxton-Hicks. She wrenched away.

"Antonio—" she panted.

"I can hardly wait to get you to my hotel," he said seductively, cupping her cheek. "Tonight, I'll show you how much I love you. Now and forever..."

Looking down, she gasped, "All that's going to have to wait."

He pulled back with a frown. "Why?"

Hana looked up, her expression in shock. "Because my water just broke!"

* * *

The cherry trees were newly in bloom when they returned to Tokyo in late March for Ren and Emika's wedding.

It had been a joyful day, full of love and laughter, tradition and cake. As they left the reception, Antonio held his wife's hand as he pushed their baby daughter's stroller. His heart was full of joy. Everywhere he looked, cherry flowers were popping like popcorn on trees, pink-and-white petals trailing in the soft spring breeze like confetti.

"Where are you taking me?" Hana asked him for the tenth time.

"It's a surprise," he told her, also for the tenth.

"Back to the plane, to take us home to Madrid?"

"No."

She blinked, then tilted her head. "To New York, then," she guessed. "So I can help you get a better deal this time."

She never let him forget how he'd gotten hosed in the union deal he'd made without her. A mistake he'd never been stupid enough to make again. From now on, they were partners all the way. At work. And at home. Smiling, he shook his head.

"Where?" she begged.

He grinned. "Come with me."

As he led her down the Tokyo street, Antonio's shoulders became a little straighter. He was filled with pride to have his wife on his arm, and pushing his baby daughter in the stroller. At five months old, Josie was already grabbing her own feet, and clearly a prodigy.

Her birth hadn't been easy. After twenty hours of labor, she'd been born finally by cesarean section in a Tokyo hospital. Every time Antonio remembered that night, he was awed by his wife's power and strength. Afterward, he'd wanted to shower her with jewels, but she'd told him his love was the only gift she ever wanted. "It's yours forever," he'd breathed, his eyes suspiciously wet.

A week later, they'd taken their baby, named Josie after his mother, back to the nursery waiting at their *palacio* in Madrid. Soon afterward, his mother had gotten a chance to meet her namesake. They had photos of their baby being held tenderly in her grandmother's lap, which would always be among their most precious possessions.

Antonio had wanted his mother to come live

in the *palacio*, where he could oversee her care. But Josune had refused. "Etxetarri is my home," she'd told him in her softly wheezing voice. "I never want to leave it." But her hand had reached helplessly toward her son.

And so, with Hana's blessing, the Delacruz family had set up housekeeping in the seaside village. They'd rented a cottage just down the cliff from the hospice, and spent time with his mother every day, reading stories aloud, playing cards, just sitting quietly. Antonio had been with her when she'd peacefully died a few weeks later, surrounded by her family, and with a loving smile on her lips.

In one of their last conversations, Josune had told Antonio how proud she was of him, what a good man he was, how much she loved him. He wasn't sure he deserved such praise. But now he was a father, he finally understood.

Because that was exactly how he felt about baby Josie. Every time his daughter did something clever, like lifting her head or making a noise that sounded like "Papa"—something he was absolutely, positively sure she was doing deliberately, no matter how doubtful Hana was about it—he felt the need to share it, to praise it, to video record it, to send it to all their friends. And even—in one particularly embarrassing incident his wife still teased him about—he couldn't help mentioning his daughter in a company email to his eleven thousand employees. His cheeks went hot remembering that one. In his defense, Josie had done something remarkably difficult, sitting up all by herself for a full thirty seconds.

"She's clearly a prodigy," he'd informed his wife. She'd laughed, then informed him that his reputation in the business world for cold, ruthless savagery had taken a hit lately.

"Everyone's starting to think you're a big softy," Hana had said, then laughed even louder at the horrified look on his face. Then he caught himself.

"It's all part of my plan to lure them in. I'm ruthless as ever," Antonio replied smugly. "Trust me."

And he was ruthless. In business, when he wanted to be. But always, always ruthless about showing his family how much he loved them.

Now, in the two days they had to spend in Tokyo before they returned home to Madrid, Antonio wanted to do something for his wife.

She didn't care about money. She didn't care about jewels. But she'd told him once about something she wanted.

As Antonio pushed their baby's stroller beneath the warm spring sunshine, he led her to the best park in Shinjuku for cherry tree viewing. He'd already arranged a blanket to be set up. On top of it, a wicker basket was waiting for them.

"What's this?" she asked, her forehead furrowed.

"A family picnic," he said. "Beneath the cherry trees." He spoke the Japanese word, just as his buddy Ren Tanaka had helped him practice. *"Hanami."*

Her lips parted in shock. "Your accent—it's perfect!"

Stopping beside the blanket, beneath the largest, most beautiful pink cherry tree against the bright blue sky, he parked the stroller. "I want to make all your dreams come true, *querida*. As you have mine."

Hana looked astonished. "I've made your dreams come true?"

Antonio took her in his arms. "You know you have. And you do every day. Especially today."

Hana blushed. She trembled. Then she whispered, "How did you know?"

"You told me last year that…" Then he blinked. "Wait. What are you talking about?"

Blushing, she ducked her head, her long dark hair falling in soft waves over her pale pink trench coat. "You said I made your dreams come true, especially today. So I thought…"

"Thought what?"

Shaking her head shyly, she gave him a slow-rising smile. "I thought you'd somehow found out…" Rising on her tiptoes, she whispered in his ear. He drew back. Now he was the one to look astonished.

"I just confirmed it at the doctor's before the wedding this morning. I heard the heartbeat." Her smile lifted to a saucy grin. "Heart*beats*."

His eyes went wide. "Are you saying—?"

"Twins," she said happily.

With a cry of joy, he pulled her into his arms and kissed her again and again.

She laughed. "If we keep having babies at this rate, Josie will soon be part of a baseball team. You don't mind?"

"Sounds like paradise." Then, remembering how hard labor had been for her, he asked softly, "You're not afraid?"

Hana tilted her head. "I'll have more scars." She put her hand over her dress, over her belly with its cesarean scar. Then she smiled. "But that's all right. It's *kintsugi*." She looked up at him, her eyes luminous. "Do you remember?"

Antonio's heart was full. "How could I forget? It's the scars that make things truly beautiful." Cupping her cheek, he looked into her face. "Even more beautiful than when they were new."

Hana's eyes widened, and he saw she was surprised he'd remembered. But he'd never heard anything so accurately explain what life should be.

He looked around them. Cherry blossoms were blooming again. Soon, they'd disappear. But every year, they came back. That was the beauty of life, the promise, the renewal. He'd lost so much in his life. But how much more had he gained?

As Antonio curled into the soft blanket beneath the pink flowering tree, with his chortling baby in his lap and his newly pregnant wife resting her head on his shoulder, he knew that everything he'd lost was a tiny fraction, the merest drop of water, compared to the Pacific Ocean of happiness all around him. And as he kissed his wife tenderly on the forehead, he knew broken hearts, mended and made new, were the strongest and most powerful of all.

* * * * *

LET'S TALK
Romance

For exclusive extracts, competitions
and special offers, find us online:

 facebook.com/millsandboon

@millsandboonuk

@millsandboon

Or get in touch on 0844 844 1351*

For all the latest titles coming soon,
visit millsandboon.co.uk/nextmonth